ELEMENTS OF CHOICE

Iris L Curtis

A PSYCHOLOGICAL THRILLER

Copyright © [2017] by [Iris L Curtis]
All rights reserved.
ISBN: 978-1673481549

This is a work of fiction. Names, characters, organisations and incidences are either a product of the author's imagination or used fictitiously.

No part of this book may be reproduced without prior consent of the author

Dedicated to Ted, with much love and grateful thanks for reading early drafts and still having faith in me!

Much love also to Simon, Mark and Robin and their families

***

With special appreciation to:

Mark for producing another stunning cover

Trish, who continually inspires
me to keep writing

'The Tiara Writing Group' for their
constructive critiquing

Leo, whose creative writing course gave
me the idea for my main character

ALSO BY THE SAME AUTHOR:

Deception & Lies

Twins Heather and Lucy set up a fashion company and just as the business is taking off, Lucy discovers her husband Tom is having an affair.

Is Heather sleeping with Tom? Believing it to be true, Lucy fires her sister and hires Bobbie, an eccentric PA, to help run the expanding company.

The twins eventually reconcile, but disaster strikes and an opportunity opens for the still resentful Heather to become her charismatic twin; but can she convince Bobbie who has escalating problems of her own to resolve.

Meanwhile Tom continues to stir up trouble, unaware of the devastating consequences of his meddling that no one could have foreseen.

***

ELEMENTS OF CHOICE

Martin was experiencing a rare sense of well-being as he walked up the beach after his swim.

The sea had been exhilarating and July holidaymakers, who used bags and windbreaks to mark out their territory, no longer irritated him. Instead he felt a strange flicker in the pit of his stomach as if something exciting was about to happen.

Hot sand scorched his feet so he was glad to step onto the ground sheet he'd laid out earlier and it was only as he started to towel himself down that he spotted her, sitting on a blanket behind two boys who were building a sandcastle. Then one kid hit out at the other with his spade and both ran off leaving nothing but a pile of sand between them.

She must have sensed she was being watched because she stopped rubbing cream into her legs and turned, the look of uncertainty followed swiftly by a warm smile.

'Martin ... I wondered if I'd see you ... How's it going, then?'

'Oh ... um ... okay. Nothing much changes round here; you still working in London?'

Martin kicked at the abandoned castle and Alison's smile slipped as she twitched her legs away, a fraction too late to avoid the shower of damp sand. Recovering quickly, she pulled a wet wipe from her bag and dabbed at the grit while describing her high-powered job in a city bank; but, he wasn't listening.

Last time they'd seen each other was two years ago, at her fiancé's funeral, and this was a very different girl from the one who'd moved to the capital shortly afterwards. Now, the tousled hair was streaked with highlights and she was wearing make-up, something she would never have done on the beach before. A dolphin, tattooed just above her right ankle, was also new and she had an air about her that made Martin feel provincial.

'... so, yes ... still working in the city,' Alison concluded. 'And I got a promotion recently, which was great.' She waited. Then, smiling encouragingly, asked, 'How about you ... What have you been up to?'

To his relief, Martin was spared the embarrassment of discussing his mundane life when Alison caught sight of an older man heading towards them.

'Richard!' Her face lit up as she jumped to her feet and ran over to link arms as they walked back together. 'Martin, this is my fiancé.' The dark haired stranger smiled down on her as she added, 'I've brought him over for the weekend to meet my parents.'

Later, watching them saunter off hand in hand, Martin wondered what she saw in the new future husband. Surely it wasn't money; the Alison he remembered would never be influenced by wealth; and it couldn't be looks - the first one had been younger and certainly more handsome.

Coincidences didn't exist in Martin's world. There had to be a reason for their paths to cross again and he followed at a distance, unable to stop himself revisiting the dream where Alison was permanently back in his life.

CHAPTER 1

The next morning Martin sat by the window of a seaside cafe, enjoying a full English breakfast. Engrossed in a Motoring magazine, he didn't notice Alison breeze in as he mopped up the last bit of egg with a slice of fried bread and jumped in surprise when she took the seat opposite, her perfume mingling with the breakfast smells.

'Hi Martin; what are you up to today? Not working, I hope. It's so lovely out there.'

'No, I'm off now 'til Monday... ' Martin flushed under her gaze. 'I'll probably go for a swim; ... see where the day takes me...'

'Sounds like a great idea,' Alison's eyes sparkled across the table. 'I was thinking of doing the same myself.'

'Well ... um ... you could always come with me ... that is, if you want to?'

'Thanks, I'd love to,' she smiled and Martin caught his breath when she added, 'Shall I get my things and meet you by the clock? .... Say around ten thirty?'

'Okay ... and maybe we could get some lunch afterwards ... only if you've got time, of course.'

But Alison, ignoring interest from both sides

of the counter, was already heading for the door. 'See you later,' she called and left the café, giving a wave as she went.

Oblivious to envious glances, Martin went to wave back, but instead put the magazine into his backpack and got up to leave. Did she seek him out ... or just notice him as she walked past? And, why wasn't she with the new fiancé?

In less than twenty-four hours he was as screwed up as he'd always been when Alison was around.

Later that morning, they went back to where they'd met the day before. Alison was wearing a different swimsuit and Martin watched as she spread out a large blanket before sinking down and gesturing for him to join her.

The beach was filling with tourists who could hardly believe their luck at picking such a glorious week and all around, parents were smothering protesting children in sunscreen before pulling T-shirts over their heads.

Martin scowled when a beach ball landed close by and Alison threw it back to the young guy who blushed when she wagged a finger jokingly at him. Even now, the attention she attracted got to him.

'You're probably wondering where Richard is?' Alison's smile faded as she scooped up sand, allowing the fine grains to trickle through her fingers.

Martin shrugged.

'Well, he's at a video conference this morning ... that's why he booked himself into a hotel instead of staying with me at Mum and Dad's. Amuse yourself as I'll be busy 'til this evening, he said when I went round. I complained of course, but he just said we'll have tomorrow and Sunday so go and enjoy the sunshine.'

Alison sighed. 'I just wish he'd forget about work once in a while. This was supposed to be our time. If I hadn't seen you, I'd have been stuck on my own all day.'

Martin looked to see if she'd realised how insulting that sounded and saw she hadn't. So ... self-centred as ever then.

Later, when they went for a swim, he was pleased to see she still waded into the cold waves with no hesitation or girlie shrieks and, as she powered through the water towards him, he noticed how her eyes matched the sky on the horizon.

Back on the blanket Alison chatted easily and he found himself telling her a bit about his life over the last two years - not that there was much to tell. He still worked in a garage, but at least it was a good one and, being the senior mechanic, he delegated routine repairs so he could service top of the range vehicles.

Then, Alison told him about her fiancé's new Porsche. 'It's red and does nought to sixty in three or four seconds ... whatever use that is,' she added. 'And Richard says it has a top speed of over one hundred and fifty miles an hour.' She laughed as Martin tried not to look impressed. 'Honestly, you boys and your toys. It's not as if you can ever do that on our roads. Anyway, what are you driving now?'

'Oh, still the same Ford Focus ... but, I do get to drive cars like Richard's. I prefer my own though because there's no other quite like it.'

'Yes, I remember,' smiled Alison. 'You customised it while I was here and it's very distinctive ... Sooo, how's your mum? Are you still living at home?'

'Mmm ... how are Fay and David?'

'Oh, they're fine. Mum enjoys her various committees and just generally looking after Dad ...'

When Alison - also an only child – paused and gazed out to sea, Martin knew she was picturing her parents who, in their forties, were around the same age as his mother had been when he was born.

'... And Dad's still at the Comp ... even now he's hoping I might follow him into education and end up teaching here one day.' She lay back on the blanket and adjusted her sunglasses.

'Oh yes,' Martin's pulse quickened when he saw the toned body stretched out beside him, 'and would you?'

'Oh, I don't know. I like my job and if I'm honest, I like the money. Maybe when we get married? We'll see.'

The idea of Alison marrying somebody else still appalled him and Martin searched for a subject that didn't involve Richard.

'So ... how did the London job come about?'

Alison sat up and hugged her knees. 'Well, Paul ... you remember my first fiancé? ... He worked in London as a solicitor and I applied for a transfer nearby so we could be together. I was amazed when they offered me the post because there'd been so much competition...'

She whipped off her glasses, the faraway look suggesting she hadn't thought about this in ages and Martin, who'd gone cold, knew exactly what was coming.

'Then, a week or two before I was due to start the new job, Paul found what he said was the perfect flat and came down for the weekend so he could drive me back to see it ...

'We'd booked to have dinner a few miles up the coast on the Saturday and that afternoon he walked into town to do some shopping. He said he'd be back by six to pick me up and I was surprised when he didn't show; Paul was always a stickler for punctuality; it used to annoy me sometimes ...'

The tightly pinched lips reminded Martin of times when he'd been on the receiving end of that look.

'... Anyway, it got to six-thirty so I called his mobile ... it was awful. The phone rang for ages, then a man answered and I could hardly hear him over all the noise. He told me he was a policeman and said the man who owned the phone had been hit by a car. I asked, "Is he badly hurt? Will he be okay?" But the man just said they were taking him to St. Steven's and that I'd better meet them there.'

She rummaged for a tissue while Martin shuffled uncomfortably, wanting to hear more but at the same time desperate for the story to be over; he hoped she was in too deep to notice.

'I arrived at the hospital just as they were wheeling Paul out of the ambulance and could see from their faces it was bad ...'

Martin put a tentative arm round her and thought for a moment she was trying to shake it off; then he realised she was sobbing.

'I'm so sorry,' she hiccuped, leaning into him, 'I didn't mean to drag this up, but being in Southcliffe has brought it all back. I never even got to say goodbye. Paul died on the operating table. I don't know how I got through the funeral ... did you go? I don't remember seeing you.'

'I went, but didn't get a chance to speak to you.'

As he kissed her cheek, Martin wasn't sure why he'd lied.

Later, Alison excused herself from lunch as she'd arranged to join Richard for a bite to eat in the hotel dining room.

'But, we could meet up again this afternoon.' Having recovered her composure, she treated Martin to a dazzling smile. 'Perhaps we could go for a spin round the bay. My father's still got his boat so I'm sure he'll lend it to me ... and I promise I won't break down again.' The smile was persuasive. 'Shall we meet by the Marina? ... Say in a couple of hours?'

Martin nodded.

'See you later, then.'

While Alison headed off to Richard's seafront hotel, Martin went back to the café where he tried to read his magazine and force down a sandwich, but it was impossible to concentrate on either.

Why had he allowed himself to be sucked in? There could only be one outcome and did he really want to go through all the heartache again?

He sighed. As always, where Alison was involved, he had no choice.

CHAPTER 2

Richard had been droning on about his business meeting throughout lunch, but Alison wasn't paying attention. Instead, she was seeing for the first time how the expensive clothes and Rolex watch appeared flashy against the faded grandeur of a pre-war seaside hotel. She was also realising how his love of good food, together with an interest in fine wines, had led to the beginnings of a paunch.

Having just turned thirty-two, he seemed older than local men of his age, with glossy black hair starting to grey at the temples and a permanent furrow etched into his brow from hours spent staring at computer screens.

A stockbroker by profession, he would rather have joined the police force but, much as he enjoyed the idea of solving crimes, he'd been seduced by the lure of big money; hence a stressful job in the city, which provided him with a very comfortable lifestyle and a Docklands flat.

Richard finally ran out of steam while coffee was being served and Alison took the opportunity to tell him what she'd been doing while he'd been so busy. Aware he wasn't impressed with her choice of companion – last night she'd told him they'd dated as teenagers - she seized on the one thing both men had in common.

'You'd like Martin's car,' she said, 'he customised it a few years ago and apparently it 'goes like a rocket' since he's done more work on it.' She smiled. 'You know, he's just as obsessed with his wheels as you are ... in fact he made me laugh earlier, going on about how he wouldn't be seen dead in 'an un-cool' car as he put it. But, I did see him once in a beat up old Skoda ... I was driving to the hospital on the day of Paul's accident and...'

She'd strayed into forbidden territory; Richard hated it when she talked about her first fiancé; but the response was not what she'd expected and her eyes widened as she started to make sense of the extraordinary theory he was putting forward.

'At the very least, you have to admit it was out of character,' Richard's eyes gleamed as he leaned across the table to grab her hands. 'Think about it, Alison ... see how it could be true. Those rumours you talked about ... people saying Paul's death might not have been an accident. Martin had the means and the motive ... I bet-'

'-Stop! ... Honestly, Richard, out of all the stupid things you've ever come out with, this has to be the most idiotic – and that's saying something.' Alison snatched her hands away to cover her ears. 'I'm not listening any more ... just because he was driving an old car that day ... you don't even know him.'

Used to outbursts of temper that were a match to his own, even Richard was shocked by the expression on Alison's face and he backtracked immediately. 'I'm sorry, darling. You're absolutely right, of course. I got carried away. It's probably the frustrated detective inside me-'

'-that's not good enough. You should think before you speak. I mean, really ... the idea is ridiculous.'

'Yes, of course it is and I'm sorry ... anyway, just out of interest, where did you say Paul was knocked down?'

'I didn't! If you must know, it was halfway up the hill from town ... but, Martin and I were over by then. We broke up ages before I got engaged to Paul.' She paused. 'Besides, there's no way Martin would ever do anything like that.'

'Not even if he was jealous? I saw him looking on the beach yesterday; believe me, he still has the hots for you. You must have noticed.'

'Not even if he was jealous,' snapped Alison. 'And, no I didn't notice, so don't even go there.'

Richard's gaze narrowed as his fiancée's cheeks flared. Then he drained the last of his coffee and beckoned the waitress over. 'I have to go back to work,' he said, signing for their meal with a flourish. 'What are you doing this afternoon?'

'Meeting Martin again; we're going for a trip

round the bay in Dad's boat ... remember, I pointed it out to you in the Marina yesterday?'

Preparing for an argument, Alison lifted her chin and was surprised when Richard merely nodded before retrieving his briefcase from under the table and getting up to leave.

'Okay. I'll see you later, then.' He dropped a kiss on the top of her head before walking away with rapid strides.

Everything about him is so quick, thought Alison - his walk, the impulsiveness ... and his temper. She sighed. Could she really accuse him of that when her own fuse was just as short?

And where did he get the idea that Martin still fancied her? Her heart skipped a beat when she remembered how fit he'd looked yesterday, having just come out of the sea. Yes, he'd behaved awkwardly at first – what with all that sand kicking – but, she'd not picked up that he was showing any particular interest in her.

In fact, it had been hard to believe he was the same creepy guy who'd fired off so many texts when she ended their relationship before going to uni. Then, he'd been determined not to let her go and had kept on messaging right up to the day she left. It had started again soon after Paul died and Alison was glad she'd not told any of this to Richard.

Looking at her watch, she got up from the table and gathered her things. She'd have to hurry if she wanted to change ... and she'd pick up the keys to her father's boat at the same time.

As she pushed through the hotel's revolving door, a tingle of excitement told her just how much she was looking forward to spending the afternoon with Martin.

CHAPTER 3

Martin arrived at the Marina a few minutes early and found a spot where he could see everyone as they approached.

Beneath the expressionless face, his mind was a jumble. Surely there was no way Alison would pass over a high flier like Richard for someone like him. But, she never used to care about status ... and would she have been so open earlier if she didn't feel something for him? Would she also have suggested meeting up again if she hadn't enjoyed their morning together? His thoughts whirled, making him dizzy.

Fine weather had brought out even more people and the sea was flat calm. The boat hire booth had a constant queue and Martin watched as everyone was given a life jacket to strap on before being allowed onto the water.

His heart started to beat faster when Alison came into view, carrying a large canvas bag. She'd changed into minute shorts, teamed with a white crop T-shirt that showed off her tan, and waved a bunch of keys, which presumably belonged to her father's boat.

Alison had also been lost in thought as she

walked to the Marina. She was beginning to see Richard in a new light and his suggestion that Martin might be responsible for Paul's accident had stunned her. It was so bizarre, but the thing that hurt most was his complete lack of sensitivity. Didn't he realise how traumatic that period in her life had been? Not for the first time she had a nagging doubt about the prospect of spending the rest of her life with a man who could steamroller over her feelings like that. On the other hand, Martin - now watching and waving - seemed far more appealing.

'The boat is moored a bit further down,' she said, after planting a kiss on his cheek. 'We can head off straight away if you're ready.'

Martin took the bag she held out and fell in step beside her.

'I brought food and drink so we can go round the headland to our beach on the other side and have a picnic if you like. Maybe we could swim again as well.'

'Sounds great,' Martin's insides had lurched once at the touch of her lips and again when she mentioned 'our' beach. Now they'd get some proper time together.

Jumping into the boat, Alison took the controls while Martin cast off and then they were skimming over the waves, the seashore and Marina morphing into the picture postcard scene that was on sale everywhere in town.

After steering skilfully round the headland,

Alison revved the engine to gather speed. Then, as the shoreline drew close, they instinctively fell into the old routine and pulled the boat onto the sand, securing it to a large rock.

'Phew, it's warm here,' said Alison, looking round for a shady spot to lay out the blanket. 'What a perfect afternoon. I really miss the sea when I'm in London, especially on a day like today. Shall we swim now and have a picnic later?'

Not trusting himself to speak, Martin nodded as he headed towards the sea while Alison stripped off to reveal a hot pink bikini, which emphasised her curves.

Still unsure of her motives, Martin kept his distance while they swam, but she gravitated towards him each time he struck out and he was just about to reverse tactics when she started to wade back to the beach.

'Come on, I'm getting hungry,' she called. 'I'll race you to the blanket.'

'Oh, that's not fair,' protested Martin. 'You cheated.'

After two or three powerful strokes he was only a couple of metres behind her on the sand when they both stopped and turned to the sound of an outboard motor.

'It's one of the hire boats,' said Martin, squinting against the sun. 'What the hell is it doing here? They're supposed to stay in the cordoned off area.' His face darkened. Bloody holidaymakers; why can't they stick to the rules?

'I thought only locals knew about this beach,' said Alison, shading her eyes. 'Whoever it is doesn't have a clue what they're doing. 'Hey, watch out!' she yelled, 'keep to your right.' She swooped with her hand and pointed as she ran past Martin towards the sea.

Swearing under his breath, Martin followed shouting and pointing until the man at the controls veered sharply just before running the boat onto the shore.

'You idiot, you must have missed the rocks by millimetres. You're not supposed to come out this far. What are you doing here?' Martin was helping Alison pull the boat to safety and it was only then that he recognised the occupant.

'For God's sake Richard, you nearly holed the boat,' Alison glared at her fiancé as he stepped onto the beach. 'I thought you were working. Why aren't you at the hotel?'

'Don't you think that's where I'd rather be?' Richard ran a shaky hand through his hair. 'I only came because your mother wanted to get a message to you.'

'Mum? ... Why, what's happened?'

'No, no, it's nothing like that,' Richard fumbled with the straps of his life jacket and threw it on the bottom of the boat. 'She just needs you to make a decision about the wedding venue. The hotel you really like has asked for a firm commitment by four o'clock ... otherwise, we may lose it to another couple.'

'What! ... Well, why didn't she phone me?'

'She couldn't get through so she rang me and I tried ... then, when you didn't pick up, I told Fay I'd try and catch you at the Marina, but you'd already left.'

'How on earth did you know I was here?'

'You said you were going for a boat trip so I asked the boat hire man and he said he'd seen two people going round the headland. Assuming it was probably you, I took out one of his boats and nipped under the ropes when he wasn't looking. Then I spotted your dad's boat ... and here I am.' Richard looked at his watch. 'It's nearly three already, but if you head straight back you should make it in time. Perhaps Martin could stay and help me, as I'm obviously not much of a sailor.' He smiled apologetically.

'But Richard ... I really don't see-'

'-darling, you know your mum's been nagging you to make up your mind; remember how last night she said they were getting impatient for a decision?'

'Yes, but not that impatient, surely-'

'-don't worry about your things. We'll bring them back with us.' Richard had started to guide her smoothly towards to the shoreline. 'Just get going, otherwise you won't make it.' He pressed forward, leaving her no choice but to climb into her father's boat, which he pushed out to sea.

'I'm sorry Martin. Are you okay with that?'

The engine sprang to life as Alison turned the key.

Martin hadn't uttered a word since Richard began his crazy story and grunted in reply. Then, while Richard waved Alison off, he went up the beach to check her phone. There was a strong signal and no missed calls so what was going on? And why hadn't he gone back with Alison.

Despite being on his guard as he returned to the water's edge, Martin was still stunned when Richard turned on him as soon as the boat disappeared from view.

'Right Martin, now I don't like you and I suspect the feeling is mutual, so let's not waste time pretending otherwise.'

Martin blinked. Surely, he hadn't come all this way to fight. But, it was Richard's next words that really set him reeling.

'What I want to know is: what were you doing on the day Paul was killed?'

Martin stared at the second man to steal Alison from him.

'I thought so.' Richard smacked a fist into his hand. 'It **was** you. You were in a beat up Skoda that evening and Alison said you never drive old cars. You staged a 'hit-and-run' to stop her marrying him, didn't you?'

Outwardly calm, Martin could feel his heart thumping as he tried to get his head round Richard's allegation. 'I have no idea what you're talking about,' he said, 'The garage takes cars in part-exchange, but that Skoda was only fit for scrap so I was taking it to the breakers yard.'

'Then, there'll be paperwork to prove it. ... And, how is it you can remember exactly which car you were driving that day? ... Oh yes, and why didn't you delegate the job to a junior mechanic, like you usually do?'

Martin's cheeks flared as he realised they must have been discussing him over lunch. 'That's some accusation,' he snarled, 'and you seem to have gone to an awful lot of trouble to make it. I assume there is no wedding emergency.'

'Too right, there isn't. I knew you were responsible for Paul's accident as soon as Alison told me about the Skoda ... and you haven't denied it.'

Martin stooped to pick up some stones and began skimming them across the water. His technique was good and even Richard was impressed as stone after stone bounced several times across the waves before plopping into the sea.

'You're out of your mind. Why would I do that? Alison and I were history long before she met Paul; everyone will tell you. What's the motive? Where's the evidence?'

'Oh, I'll find something,' Richard kicked at a pebble like a petulant schoolboy, 'anything to keep your hands off Alison.'

The next stone Martin selected was large and

smooth and with quiet deliberation, he swung it with all his strength against Richard's temple. The older man gasped, knees buckling as he dropped to the ground.

Fuelled by adrenaline, Martin hauled the unconscious body into the hired boat. A bruise was already showing, but there wasn't much blood so he scuffed over the sand where Richard had fallen, safe in the knowledge that any stray traces would soon be washed away by the rising tide. Then he flung the stone weapon out to sea and walked back to collect Alison's things. It had only been ten minutes since the boat crashed onto the beach, but it seemed a long time since they'd set out for their afternoon together.

Damn, Richard! Why did he have to interfere? And damn, Alison. Why did she have to come back and stir everything up? He'd just got his life back on track and now it was falling apart again. What had they been talking about to make him come out with such a claim?

Martin was seething as he piled everything into the boat. Then he saw Richard's mobile glinting in the sun and, after confirming there'd been no recent outgoing calls, put the phone in his pocket to show Alison.

He knew exactly what he was going to do now and, steering away from the beach, started to put his story together.

CHAPTER 4

As Alison passed the boat hire booth on her way home, she noticed it was facing away from where she'd come. So how could the man have seen them go out - especially as he'd been so busy?

She should never have allowed herself to get swept along by Richard's story. If only she'd stood her ground and insisted on calling her mother from the beach; but, as always, he'd pushed her, quite literally, into doing what he wanted her to do.

He must have hired the boat to break up her afternoon with Martin – she'd told him how lovely the beach round the headland was so he'd have assumed they'd go there - but why the pretence? He'd sounded fine about it at lunchtime.

Alison gasped and stopped so suddenly that a man walking behind nearly crashed into her. He turned to glare, but she didn't notice. Surely Richard wouldn't be that stupid?

The only way to prove his story was to speak to her mother so she started to run and ten minutes later, arrived home to find the house empty. Heading straight for the phone, she punched in Richard's number, but the call cut out after a couple of rings. Why didn't he pick up? Was he realising now how brainless he'd been?

Still out of breath, Alison went over to the kitchen sink and splashed cold water over her face, just as Fay came in from the garden.

'I thought I'd wash a duvet. It should dry quickly in this weather. Why are you back so early ... you look like a beetroot ... surely, you haven't been running in this heat?'

'Mum, did you see Richard earlier?'

'Well, he was here ... just after you picked up the boat keys. I'm surprised you didn't see him yourself.'

'We must have just missed each other. Did he say why he came?'

'Not really. I explained how you'd gone out for the afternoon, but he didn't seem surprised.

'Oh, by the way the hotel you like on the sea front left a message this morning. They asked if we could firm up a date by four o'clock tomorrow as another couple are interested now. I told Richard and he looked almost pleased; then he left without another word ... He can be quite off-hand at times, can't he?'

Alison rolled her eyes. 'He has his moments. Did he tell you where he was going?'

'No, he just went ... I have to say it was a bit odd ...'

Alison turned away to hide her anger. Thank goodness she hadn't told her mother the whole story. Then she'd have thought him more than a bit strange.

'You said you were taking the boat out,' said Fay. 'Did you change your mind?'

'I did go out for a while and put the keys back on the hook when I came in.'

'And Alison, talking of weddings, you really do need to start making some decisions...'

But Fay was talking to herself. Alison had seen a new side to Richard and cringed when she thought back to how he'd spoiled her afternoon with Martin.

At this moment, the choice of wedding hotel was the last thing on her mind.

***

When Martin heard the burst of modern jazz, he realised he should have switched Richard's mobile off; now, keeping the phone might mean he'd have to explain the unanswered call. He must eliminate complications so he threw the mobile into the sea and, just as the ripples died away, the in-shore lifeboat came spluttering towards him. Getting to his feet, he raised his arms into a diving stance.

'Stop!' The voice through a loud hailer echoed clear and urgent across the waves. 'Do not enter the water ... I repeat, don't go in the water. The currents are strong and you'll get swept away.'

Martin, who had no intention of putting his life in danger, sat down again to wait. 'I thought

I saw something,' he shouted. 'I was going to see what it was, but it's disappeared again.'

The rescue boat drew alongside and a man wearing oilskin trousers secured it to the hire boat. 'It's far too dangerous to swim here,' he warned, 'so don't even think about it. You said on the phone your friend had gone overboard and banged his head as he fell.'

'Yes. That's right.' Martin jerked a thumb over his shoulder. 'He stood on that seat and lost his balance as we came round the headland. I went straight back to pick him up, but he must have knocked himself out because he never came up.'

'How long ago did this happen?'

'About twenty minutes, I think. We were returning from the beach over there.' Deciding to stick to the truth where he could, Martin looked back the way he'd come. By his reckoning, Richard's body was well away from any search area and would probably be washed up further along the coast on the next tide.

A second crewman pointed to the yellow bundle lying on the floor of the boat. 'Please, don't tell me that's his lifejacket.'

'I did try to get him to put it on - especially as Richard can't swim - but he's very stubborn. He said the sea was calm and it wasn't necessary.'

'Why do people underestimate the dangers? Anyway, what were you doing this far out? And you ... why aren't you wearing one?'

Martin relayed the essence of Richard's story and gave an edited version of events after Alison left in her father's boat. 'It all happened so quickly and my lifejacket got left in the boat I came over in.'

'Well, you'd better put that one on now and take the boat back to the Marina.' The first lifeboat man looked at him more closely. 'You're local aren't you? Are you okay to do that?'

Martin nodded and strapped on the jacket.

'Good. We'll stay and search the area.' With hands resting on hips, he swayed to the movement of the boat and gazed round the empty sea. Then he blew out his cheeks before adding, 'you do understand it's not looking good for your friend, don't you?'

Martin lowered his eyes and nodded again.

'Okay ... well, I'll radio in to get the helicopter over in case we miss something ... and the police will need a statement so there'll be someone waiting at the Marina to speak to you when you get back.' The crewman separated the boats and they sped away to begin the search.

Martin watched them move further and further away from the spot where he'd tipped Richard's unconscious body overboard. Then he restarted the hire boat.

So far, so good; humming softly under his breath, he steered towards the Marina and smiled when he realised it was the theme from 'Jaws' that had come into his head.

***

Alison stepped into the warm sunshine and closed the front door behind her, cutting off the voice of her mother who was still going on about wedding arrangements. Richard and Martin would probably be back by now so she'd go down to the Marina to look for them. First though, she'd talk to the boat hire man and check if he'd really seen her father's boat go out earlier.

As she approached the booth, she saw a policeman talking to the hire man, who was helping a returning tripper to remove his son's lifejacket; the boy's pale body contrasting sharply with his sunburned face.

The hire man threw the jacket into a box just as another boat chugged in and the policeman went to meet the man who climbed out onto the beach.

When Alison saw it was Martin, clutching a bundle of clothes and hitching her bag higher on his shoulder, her heart started racing. Where was Richard?

Martin was already following the officer out of the Marina at a brisk pace so she sprinted over to the hire man and grabbed his arm. 'What's happened,' she gasped. 'Why did he go off with a policeman and where's the man who should have been with him?'

The hire man stepped back in alarm. 'Whoa,

steady on. What's it to you? D'you know that man?'

'Yes, of course I do ... why else would I be asking? My fiancé should have been with him ... there hasn't been an accident, has there?'

The man looked away. 'I'm sorry ... look, I really think you should talk to the police ... the boat was taken way beyond the boundaries and the area is very clearly roped-'

'-why, do I need to talk to the police?' Alison eyes were blazing as she went to catch hold of the man's arm again, but he stepped away and they both turned to the sound of the returning lifeboat, now pulling into shore a few metres away.

With heart still pounding, she ran towards the man wrapped in a blanket, who was being helped out of the boat. He was holding the side of his head with one hand while gesturing with the other and a crewman was doing his best to calm him down.

'You had a very lucky escape, Sir. The ambulance will be here in a minute, but as for your allegation, you'll need to make it official, if you're serious.'

'Don't you worry, I will. A man just tried to kill me and I'm not going to let that pass.' Richard spat the words out then turned to his fiancée. 'Ah, Alison; that precious friend of yours tried to drown me.'

The crewman raised his eyebrows. 'He's had

a bang on the head and isn't making a lot of sense at the moment. Perhaps you could shed some light?'

When Alison shook her head, he added, 'There appear to be conflicting stories. Looks like the police will have to sort this one out.'

'Hello! I am here,' Richard waved a hand in front of the man's face. 'I've told you what happened, but you don't seem to have understood.'

Alison winced at the sarcasm, but the crewman didn't react.

'We found you clinging to a rock with a bruise on your head ... and you were a long way from where you fell so the current must have carried you there. It's fortunate the tide was coming in; otherwise you'd have been dragged out to sea.'

'The current didn't take me anywhere. I swam to that rock. And it wasn't far from where I fell in.'

'Not according to the other guy ... but, the police are going to meet you in A&E so you can tell them your version from the hospital. Ah, here's the ambulance now.' The crewman looked relieved as he directed Richard towards the vehicle and helped him in.

'Can I go with him?' asked Alison and, after a nod from one of the paramedics, she followed Richard into the ambulance.

Apart from the outburst when she arrived, he'd scarcely acknowledged her and Alison felt her anger mount as she remembered the made-up message that had sparked all of this off. But, maybe now wasn't the time to go into it. 'How's your head?' she asked, before realising how trite it sounded.

'How do you think?'

Discouraged from making further conversation, and unsure of how badly hurt he was, Alison forced herself to reach for Richard's hand as they made the journey to the hospital in silence.

CHAPTER 5

Despite every window being open, the police station was steaming and PC Chris Thomas envied Martin who was still wearing swimming shorts - although he had slipped on a T-shirt at the desk sergeant's request.

The officer had already decided something didn't fit the picture of a man whose friend had just drowned. Of course, the closed expression could be disguising grief, but there was also an air of detachment that gave the impression he really wasn't bothered.

'Right, Mr Landon, perhaps you would tell me what happened this afternoon.' Chris sat back in his chair and watched closely while Martin described events up until Alison left him and Richard alone.

'... then, after I collected our things, we headed back. When we got to the headland, Richard stood on the seat and said he'd seen what he thought was a seal ... you do see them sometimes,' he added and the policeman nodded.

'As the boat turned, he fell overboard. There was a thud and I think he hit his head as he went in the water...'

Chris waited while Martin appeared to be struggling to hold back the tears.

'I went straight back to pick him up, but he'd disappeared...' The voice dropped to a whisper, 'and that's when I called the Coastguard.'

'I see...'

At that point another policeman came into the room and handed his colleague a piece of paper.

Chris read the note and frowned. 'Well, you'll be pleased to hear your friend has been found and is okay. He's in A&E at the moment, but apparently isn't badly hurt. His guardian angel must have been on the ball today.' The officer's eyes narrowed when he saw the colour drain from Martin's face. 'Are you all right? That's good news, isn't it?'

'Yyes, of course it is,' gasped Martin. 'I really thought I'd never see him again. I'd better go straight over.'

'Well, there's just one problem,' said Chris. 'It seems his memory of what happened is different from yours ... but that may be down to his injuries. I'm sure we can clear things up, but for the moment I must ask you to wait here. Would you like a drink? Tea ... coffee ... water?'

Martin's heart hammered as he paced the small interview room. It wasn't possible. Richard couldn't swim ... Alison had said ... and even if he could, how did he escape the currents?

Aware that the policeman would be back any minute, he sat down and went over his story again. It was logical. He'd even smeared Richard's blood on the edge of the boat where he could have hit his head. Surely that would convince forensics should the police decide to investigate further.

Martin flinched as another thought occurred. Would Richard mention Paul's 'hit and run?' There was nothing to support the allegations he'd made, but his mother would be very upset if she thought he'd been linked to that particular incident.

***

While Martin stewed in the police interview room, PC Mike Bolton was sweltering in a windowless area in A&E where the air-conditioning had broken down and, despite several fans, it was very oppressive. He looked at his watch and saw it had just ticked into overtime, the only compensation for being cooped up on such a lovely afternoon.

Richard had been taken to an examination room half an hour earlier and a harassed looking nurse hurried over to say they were waiting for a doctor, but the likelihood was he'd be given the all clear and allowed to leave.

'Has he calmed down?'

Mike smiled when the nurse pulled a face.

'I wish. The girl's his fiancée and if I were her, I'd be seriously considering my options. Talk about rude.'

'Maybe it's down to the head wound?'

The nurse shook her head. 'If you ask me he's paranoid; keeps going on about how someone tried to kill him and saying he wants to go back to the city.'

'Which city?'

'London, I think.' She headed back to the treatment room and took a deep breath before opening the door to check on her patient.

Mike caught a brief glimpse of a man lying on the bed while the girlfriend sat holding his hand. Then the door shut.

Typical Londoner! Mike, a local lad, had only been to the capital a couple of times - once on a school trip and once to see a show – but, the vibrancy had passed him by on each occasion. He must try to stay objective, but people like Richard really got under his skin; acting like they were above everyone else and making out they knew it all.

It felt strange being here during the day. Mike's visits usually followed urgent night-time requests to restore order in what often looked more like a war zone than a hospital department. Then the place was a powder keg and Mike raised an eyebrow at a notice on the wall saying staff would not tolerate abuse. Try telling that to someone off their face on booze or drugs at two o'clock in the morning.

Nothing of that nature today, though. Opposite, a little girl in a swimsuit sat on her mother's lap with a blood stained towel wound round her foot. Her face was streaked with dried tears as she chewed on a chocolate bar from the machine. When she looked across he smiled, but she turned away, burying her head in her mother's shoulder.

A couple of seats away an elderly couple chatted quietly. The woman had a cast on her arm and they obviously hadn't trusted the forecast as both carried sweaters in case it turned cooler. Not a chance on a day like today, thought Mike.

Ten minutes later the waiting room had emptied and Mike was getting restless when Richard emerged with Alison a couple of paces behind.

A different nurse came over. 'He's all yours,' she said, 'and he's been discharged so is free to go when you've finished with him.'

'Thanks. Is there a room we could use for a few minutes? I don't think this will take long.'

But, he was wrong. Richard meant business and no way was Mike going to wrap things up here. 'I think we'd better go to the police station after all,' he suggested when Richard started to get heated again. 'You can give a statement there. I assume you want to press charges.'

'Too right, I do. And, there's another matter I want to raise as well regarding that man.'

Alison caught hold of his arm. 'Richard, you

can't ... You took a chance remark and blew it up out of all proportion.'

'That's what you say. I happen to think differently.' Richard shook Alison off and started to walk away.

'Do you want to come with us?' Mike, following after, turned to Alison who had not moved. 'I could drop you somewhere if it helps.'

'No thanks. I think I'll walk.'

CHAPTER 6

Richard had asked Mike to stop off at the hotel so he could change into dry clothes and, on arrival at the police station, he'd nearly refused the offer of refreshments, but changed his mind when he realised it would buy him time to pull his thoughts together. Now, while waiting for the officer to return with coffee, he was unaware that Martin was being held in a similar interview room on the opposite side of the corridor.

It had been a really bad idea to follow Alison; her reaction when he crashed onto the beach had said it all; and, as he'd watched her head back to the Marina, he suspected she'd soon be sailing out of his life in the same way. Being rude on the way to A&E hadn't improved things, but he'd been so angry, he couldn't help himself.

Now though, he had another more pressing problem because the period between watching Alison disappear round the headland and being jolted back into consciousness by icy water was a complete blank; although he knew instinctively Martin was responsible.

The doctor had explained how temporary amnesia wasn't unusual after a head injury and advised him to have further checks if it didn't resolve; but, for the moment, everyone would believe Martin's story unless he could prove otherwise. The police would need a motive before taking him seriously and, when they discovered Martin had never even heard of Richard until yesterday, his argument would lose all credibility.

Also, although he hated to admit it, Alison was right about not bringing up Paul's accident. If he couldn't convince them that Martin had harmed him today, why would they consider reopening a two-year old road accident case on his say so? The more he thought about it, the more futile it all seemed.

***

'What's going on?' Martin's officer had caught up with Mike who was in the corridor, carrying two mugs of coffee.

'Don't ask.' Mike glanced towards the room where Richard was waiting. 'The guy in there thinks someone tried to kill him ... but I think a bang on the head sent him loopy,' Mike scowled as he remembered Richard's behaviour at the hospital, 'Not that he wasn't loopy to start with ... being from London.'

Chris grinned, well aware of Mike's distrust of anything to do with the capital. 'I've spoken to the other fellow and his version sounds more likely. He said your man fell in the sea when the boat turned and you know what the currents are like out there. He could easily have been swept the few hundred metres to where he was found so the only wonder is, he didn't drown on the way.'

'Well, I'm about to take a statement,' said Mike. 'Do you want to sit in?'

As they entered the room, Richard got to his feet. 'I've been thinking,' he muttered, not meeting Mike's eye, 'I don't want to press charges. I just want to forget the whole business and go home.'

The officers exchanged glances and Mike frowned. 'Are you sure? You were determined at the hospital ... and you also said there was another matter you wanted to raise-'

'-yes, I know; but, I've changed my mind. I'm entitled to do that aren't I?' Richard gave the policeman a belligerent stare.

Mike took a deep breath. 'Hold on, Mr Clancy, I've spent half the afternoon waiting to get a statement from you and now you say you've had second thoughts. Well, there may just be the matter of wasting police time...'

Chris touched his colleague's arm, eyes flicking to a pile of folders by the computer in a paperwork warning. 'Perhaps in view of the head injury, we should let it go this time?' he suggested.

Mike hesitated. Then he nodded and turned to Richard. 'Think yourself lucky,' he said, coldly, 'and next time you're in a boat, wear a life jacket.'

'That won't be necessary as I doubt I'll ever go out on the sea again.' Richard stepped towards the door. 'May I go now?'

Mike and Chris moved aside to let him pass.

'Be sure of your facts before you start throwing accusations around again or you could find yourself in a lot of trouble.' Mike couldn't resist one final dig as he called after him and nodded to the duty officer who let Richard out of the building. Then he handed one of the coffees to his colleague and frowned again. 'That was a bit weird wasn't it?'

'Maybe,' Chris shrugged, 'however, I'd just be grateful you don't have to put up with him anymore.'

'Hmm ... you're probably right ... but I still think we might be missing something.'

'Well, if he doesn't want to take it further, there's nothing we can do ... aren't you on overtime?'

'Yes ... two hours and all for nothing.' Mike swallowed his coffee in one gulp before turning to the door. 'Anyway, I'm off now. See you next week.'

Walking into the evening sunshine, Mike banished all thoughts of stroppy Londoners as he began to look forward to his own weekend.

***

Richard stood outside the police station and gazed round uncertainly. Used to being in control, his world had been turned upside down and the charm of a seaside town on a beautiful summer evening eluded him. All he wanted was to go back to the city where he belonged.

His thoughts turned to Alison. Everything had changed and he had no idea if they could survive this. Where was she, anyway? Why hadn't she come with him to the police station?

He walked away slowly, but then his pace quickened as an idea formed. Alison had driven them down in her car because he'd been drinking at a business lunch. They were supposed to be stopping 'til Sunday, but Richard couldn't hang about any longer in this backwater. He checked his watch. It was still early. If he hurried, he'd have time to catch the evening train to London.

Richard broke into a jog as he pictured himself back in his own flat. Maybe when Alison returned after the weekend, she'll have missed him enough to forgive his behaviour and they would be able to put this whole disastrous day behind them. Either way, it was a chance he had to take because now the only thought in his head was to get away from here as soon as possible.

CHAPTER 7

Shortly after Richard left for the hotel, Martin emerged from the police station, still recovering from yet another big shock; but at least this one was welcome. Richard had dropped all charges and he thanked whichever deity was responsible for making him back off.

The policeman had said Richard was probably disoriented and most likely imagined the whole thing. How long have you known him, he'd asked? And, when Martin said they'd met for the first time yesterday, he'd stood to one side leaving him free to go. All in all it had been a close call though and Martin knew he'd been fortunate.

Lost in thought, he began to walk home and it took a few moments to register that someone behind was calling him. Startled, he turned to see Alison, running towards him.

'What happened?' she gasped as soon as she was within earshot.

'Well ... you won't believe this, but your fiancé was going to accuse me of attempted murder?' Martin was careful to inject both outrage and bewilderment into his reply as he handed over the canvas bag he'd brought back for her.

'What! ... Please, tell me you're joking.'

'Why would I joke about something like that? The guy's obviously got serious issues.'

'But, it doesn't add up ... you hardly know each other?' Alison rummaged in the bag for her phone.

'I told them that. Anyway, he must have realised how ridiculous it sounded because he changed his mind ... Not before I'd been held at the police station most of the afternoon, though.'

'Oh, Martin, I'm so sorry. Honestly, I don't know what got into him today. He's been behaving strangely since lunchtime. Do you know where he is now?'

'I've no idea.'

She frowned and took the phone away from her ear. 'I can't get through on his mobile; it must be in a black spot.'

'Isn't it more likely to be out there somewhere?'

Alison banged the palm of her hand on her forehead as she followed Martin's gaze. 'In the sea ... of course, why didn't I think of that? I'd better go and find him. Will you come back to the hotel with me?'

'Okay ... but only to the entrance; it's on my way anyway.'

Martin took back the bag she held out for him to carry and they started to walk.

'He was lying, you know ... when he said he'd

come with a message from Mum.'

'Oh? ... And why would he do that?'

'I don't know ... Perhaps he was jealous ... Anyway, what actually happened out there?'

Re-telling his story, Martin almost believed it himself as he concluded how Richard must have knocked himself out as he went in the water.

'Hmm ...' Alison's eyes were fixed to the ground as they approached the hotel. 'What I'm really asking is what went on after I left and before Richard fell in the sea.'

'Oh.' Martin paused. 'Well, nothing; I just packed up our things and we got in the boat to come back to the Marina.'

'Did Richard ... um ... did he say anything?'

'Only something about being sorry to spoil the afternoon...'

Alison looked up and smiled as she took his arm for the last few yards. 'Well, I'm sorry too. I was really looking forward to that picnic.'

To Martin's relief, no more questions were asked and Alison gave a sigh as she took back her bag again. 'I suppose I'd better go and see what he's doing,' she said. 'Thanks for seeing me back.'

'You'll be okay?'

'Oh, I should think so. Richard can get uptight, especially when his pride is hurt, but he's had time to calm down so I'm sure I can handle him.'

As she spoke a mini-cab came down the hotel

driveway and stopped at the gates, waiting for a break in the traffic to turn right. They crossed behind it then Alison walked towards the entrance while Martin continued on his way home.

***

Richard ducked when he saw them; then peered through the back window of the cab as it sped away from the hotel.

He knew now he'd lost Alison and the truth was she'd started to leave him the minute they arrived. She'd been so pleased to be back and he could see she was far more at home here than in London. She'd also been very annoyed about the videoconference - even though he'd told her about his work schedule when they booked the weekend.

It was typical of Alison to expect him to change his plans to suit her and she'd become even more distant after meeting Martin on the beach yesterday. Now, this afternoon's nightmare had probably destroyed anything that may have been left between them ... and the last straw would be his running out on her. She'd never forgive him for that.

When the cab pulled up outside the station, the train was waiting and Richard's pulse quickened. Much as he loved Alison, he would never sacrifice his life in the city; and he'd always suspected she would want to return at some point to be by the sea.

Ten minutes later, the train gathered speed and Richard's spirits revived as he headed back to the bustle of city life.

***

'Martin, wait for me.'

A few minutes after her leaving at the hotel, Martin turned to see Alison running towards him.

'He's gone,' she gasped. 'Just checked out and went. Why would he do that?'

Martin's knees quivered as relief flooded through him. 'Perhaps he's at your parents' house?'

Alison stabbed at her mobile before having a terse conversation with her mother. 'No, he's not been there,' she snapped, 'What time does the London train leave?'

'In about half an hour, I think ... but, why would he go back; perhaps he's just out walking?'

'Richard doesn't do 'just out walking." Alison swore under her breath as she fumbled to get the phone back in the overstuffed bag. 'I know he's left because I saw him check out the train times soon after we arrived; he hates it here. He was probably working on an escape route even then ... and Richard always cuts and runs when he's in a hole.' She flicked her hair back in another well remembered gesture. 'Anyway, the receptionist said he'd ordered a taxi.'

Alison's jaw dropped. 'Omigod ... I bet he was in the mini-cab that was leaving when we got here.'

'It looked empty to me.'

'Well, he stayed out of sight, didn't he? It must have been him.' Alison kicked out at a stone, which went spinning into the road.

'Sooo ... what do you want to do? We'd never get to the station in time, now.'

'I'm not chasing after him. If he wants to scuttle away then let him. I've just about had enough of Richard.'

Alison started to flounce off; then stopped before retracing her steps. 'Are you hungry?'

Martin, being too keyed up to eat at lunchtime ... and unable to touch their picnic earlier ... realised he was famished and nodded.

'What if we get something to eat down on the sea front? Is that nice restaurant still there? ... Or, how about fish and chips ... we could sit and eat it on the beach?' Alison was smiling now and raised her eyebrows in a question.

'Fish and chips on the beach, sounds great.'

'Fish and chips it is, then.'

Alison took Martin's arm and once again he carried her bag, marvelling at the way she was still able to change mood in a nanosecond when it suited her.

CHAPTER 8

Alison had reluctantly declined Martin's suggestion that they might meet up the next day. I need to think things through and must spend some time with Mum and Dad, she'd explained. I've hardly seen them since we came down.

Supper on the beach had been unexpectedly lovely and Alison had gone to bed with her thoughts spinning. Richard had transformed from charming and self-assured to bullying and insensitive; he'd also lied and, despising her hometown, taken no trouble to hide it, even in front of her parents. In contrast, Martin had changed from a scary stalker into being mature and likeable.

Before she fell asleep, Alison knew she would break off the engagement.

The next day she found her parents drinking coffee and enjoying the morning sunshine in the garden.

'You don't sound very surprised,' she said, after telling them her decision and explaining how Richard had gone back to London.

'Well, love, he may be rich and have good prospects, but neither of us felt he was right for you.' Fay met Alison's gaze from under her sun visor. 'Don't look so shocked. You must have noticed how uncomfortable he was with us.'

Alison glanced over to her father who was nodding in agreement. 'But, why isn't he right ... and why did you only just think to tell me?'

Fay reached for her daughter's hand. 'Oh, darling, how could we say anything while Richard was here? You'd have chewed our heads off. But you gave it away when you couldn't decide on a wedding venue. I knew you weren't really sure when you didn't grab the hotel on the sea front. You've always said you would want to get married there.'

Alison's mouth fell open. For as long as she could remember, her mother had been able to home straight to the heart of any situation and lay it bare for her to see. 'But, you still haven't said why he isn't right for me,' she snapped.

'Well, for a start he hates it here and you'd have found that very difficult; especially if you decide to have a family. You'd want your children to have the same freedom you had as a child and that would be more difficult in London.'

Her father cleared his throat and chipped in. 'Also, we didn't like the way he treated you. He was disrespectful and we both think you deserve better than that.'

Alison's face reddened as the truth hit home. 'Well, why didn't you say so? Were you just going to let me make the biggest mistake of my life?

Doesn't my happiness mean anything to you?'

'Really, darling, can you honestly say you'd have taken the slightest bit of notice? You'd have told us to mind our own business ... and rightly so because you had to find it out for yourself. Besides, we could see it was only a matter of time before you realised. The only surprise is that it took as long as it did.'

Alison was silent.

'Sit down and have a cup of coffee.' David drew another chair out from the table while Fay went off to the kitchen. 'We haven't seen anything of you since you got here.'

Alison dropped onto the seat and sighed. 'Oh, Dad, everything's gone wrong. What am I going to do?' She folded her arms on the table and rested her head.

David stroked his daughter's hair. 'It feels like the end of the world now, but you'll see in time it's for the best.'

Alison sat up and glared at her father who raised his hands in submission. 'I know, I know,' he continued.' It's not what you want to hear, but trust me; you'll see I'm right, once things have settled down.'

Fay returned with the coffee and sat down, tipping her head away from the sun while gesturing for David to adjust the parasol. 'What happened to make you change your mind?' she asked.

'Oh, I don't know ... but I do know you're

right.' Alison's energy levels had drained to a point where she was unable to sustain her anger. 'I'm so glad I brought him down here. He was very different in London.'

'I think it's time you thought about what you really want,' said David, 'You've been in London two years now and carved out a good career, but is it going to satisfy you, long term ... especially now you're single again?'

All at once, the full force of Richard leaving hit Alison like a punch to the stomach; the impact being so hard, she could almost feel air being driven out of her body. Her father's concerned face blurred behind an onrush of tears and, not wanting to break down in front of her parents, she jumped up and shouted over her shoulder that she was going out.

Stopping only to pick up her phone and fill a water bottle, she got into her car and drove off, heading inland to avoid the possibility of bumping into Martin.

Having parked and paid, Alison set off on the five-mile circular trek she remembered doing as a child with her parents. While she walked, she allowed her mind to wander. Did she want to stay in corporate banking? More to the point, did she want to remain in London?

Poor Dad, she thought, he'd be so happy if I went into teaching and got a job at the Comp. And the truth was, in London there'd been no time to think of anything other than work. Did she really want to go back to that ... especially now Richard was out of her life?

Getting into her stride, Alison could feel the tension ebbing away. The regular pad, pad of her trainers on the soft track, together with the bump, bump of the backpack on her shoulders was soothing and without meaning to, Alison found her thoughts drifting to the darkest period of her life.

Yesterday, when she'd told Martin about Paul's death, it had brought everything back and she realised now that it was the first time she'd allowed herself think about it.

She shuddered at the awfulness... of listening while her father phoned on her behalf to offer condolences to his parents ... of choosing something suitable to wear at the funeral ... of facing up to life without Paul.

Then, there'd been the tears of mourners, which flowed while hymns were sung and, in her mind's eye, she saw the crematorium curtains close round the coffin before it went on its final journey. But, she'd stayed dry-eyed throughout and Alison had suspected that people were wondering about her lack of emotion.

How had she stayed so detached? She'd really loved Paul and should have been in pieces, but she knew now she must have been in denial because although she'd seen and heard everything, her brain had likened it to a movie. She'd even focused on the outfit of Paul's cousin at one point and wondered where the girl had bought it. The memory appalled her.

After the funeral, she'd gone to London to start her new job and within a week was living in one room of a big house that had been converted into bed-sits. There were three other lodgers, all single girls, and they'd shared the kitchen and bathroom.

Initially, and out of character for her, Alison had kept her distance, but one of the girls had been persistent. Why don't you come out with us this evening? She'd said and that was the start. Before long they all became friends, calling themselves: 'The Bed-Sit Four.' Alison smiled as she walked. What were they doing now?

Perhaps she should get in touch. She hadn't seen any of them since she moved in with Richard.

After crossing a stile, she followed an overgrown footpath along the side of a field and wondered whether the café they used to visit was still there. Recalling a badly sprained ankle that her mother suffered during one of these rural walks, she watched out for rabbit holes as her thoughts moved forward to the day she'd met Richard at the bank, a few months earlier.

He'd come in with a query and she'd been called to the floor to deal with the problem, which had arisen from an error made by the bank; but it was easily put right and he was charming and understanding about it.

He'd called back later that day to invite her out for a drink. She'd hesitated, but he wouldn't take no for an answer. Come on, he'd said, laying a persuasive hand on her arm. What have you got to lose? I promise I'm not 'the mad axe-murderer' and we can go somewhere with lots of people so you can shout for help if you're worried. He'd smiled disarmingly and they'd met after work at the wine bar over the road.

From there they'd gone to a restaurant and before she knew it they were seeing each other every night. She'd moved in with him a few weeks later and, shortly after, he'd asked her to marry him. She was still not really sure why she'd said yes as they had very little in common... apart from fantastic chemistry in bed!

Remembering the way Richard strutted rather than walked, Alison could see now how perfectly he fitted in the city ... like the centre piece of a jigsaw ... so comfortable in his own element that he hadn't enjoyed the seaside town at all. He'd hated the feel of sand on bare feet – too gritty – and, when he refused to join her for a dip in the sea, she'd put it down to him probably not being able to swim.

Having always known he would never leave the city, it hadn't bothered her as she'd no desire to move away either. But, her feelings changed when she got to Southcliffe and she had to admit it was lovely to be home again.

Alison grimaced as she narrowly missed stepping into a pile of dog poo by the kissing gate at the other end of the field. Nearly halfway through her walk, she turned down the wider path that would lead to where hopefully the café would be open. Aware now of curious glances as people passed she realised her face was wet with tears.

Then Paul's face swam into her thoughts, with his boyish smile and 'come to bed' eyes, and suddenly the floodgates opened. Blinded by tears, she stumbled to a seat and finally gave way to the grief she'd been holding on to for so long. Huge sobs racked her body and she wondered if she would ever be able to stop now she had started.

A middle-aged couple came by and went over to find out what was wrong.

'Have you been attacked, dear? Should we call the police?' The woman patted Alison's shoulder anxiously then reached into a big bag for her phone.

'No, no,' gasped Alison, 'it's nothing like that, really...' A fresh wave of despair swept over her and she sobbed like a child.

'But something must have happened,' said the man. 'Are you sure no one tried to hurt you?'

'Yes, I'm sure,' Alison hiccupped, 'I'm upset because I've just split up with my fiancé...'

It was all she was able to say coherently but, even in her despair, she thought it more plausible than admitting to crying so hard for a man who'd been dead two years. She blew her nose on a now soggy tissue and wiped her eyes with the clean one the woman handed her.

'Ah, that would explain it,' relief softened the lines on the woman's face as she delved into her bag for more tissues. 'I know just the cure for that. Well ... a diversion at any rate. We're on our way to a café that does delicious cream teas. Why don't you join us? It's a bit off the beaten track so not many people know about it.'

Her rescuers were clearly proud of how they'd discovered this 'little-known oasis' on a previous excursion so Alison didn't let on she'd been heading there herself. 'Well, if you're sure you don't mind,' she sniffed and followed the couple to the empty café where they sat at a table by the window.

'Now,' said the woman when her husband had come back from placing the order, 'I'm Marge and this is Bill. Why don't you tell us all about it; we're very good listeners.' She shot Bill a meaningful glance as his eyes glazed over. 'That is, if you think it would help,' she added, while her husband sighed and turned to stare at a pair of blue-tits pecking at a fat-ball hanging outside the window.

Alison started off hesitantly, but it was good to talk to people who didn't know her and soon she was telling them all about Richard and how he didn't belong in her world at Southcliffe. 'He was so different in London,' she sobbed, 'but, he changed the minute we arrived ... and that's when I knew there was no way he would ever agree to live by the sea.'

'But, is that what you want, dear?' Marge looked perplexed. 'You said you were really enjoying your job in London.'

'Yes I am ... but I suppose deep down I've always assumed I'd come back to Southcliffe at some point ... you know ... when we had children...'

Alison glanced away shyly, wondering if she had said too much, but Marge's eyes were shiny with interest.

'And did you talk to Richard about starting a family?' she asked. 'I mean, did he know you were thinking about babies?'

Alison thought back to conversations she'd had with Richard, but they'd all been about work – his work mainly – and she realised they'd never really talked about themselves as a couple.

'No, I don't believe he did, now you mention it,' she sighed. 'We never really discussed the future in those terms.'

'Sounds like perhaps you needed to have that conversation.' Bill, spoke for the first time as he turned back from the window. 'After all, we chaps aren't mind readers. Maybe, if you'd explained how you felt-'

'-shush,' Marge nudged Bill as Alison welled

up again. 'She's upset enough without you wading in with unhelpful comments. I expect having a family was an unspoken wish for both of them.' She raised her eyebrows questioningly. 'That was the case, wasn't it, dear?'

'No,' the tears spilled over as her voice wavered. 'Bill's absolutely right. I think I was assuming something Richard had probably never considered.'

Alison realised this time her sorrow really was for the broken relationship with Richard while Bill gave Marge a look of triumph.

'Now look what you've done,' Marge glared at her husband and started to unload the tray as their food was served.

'Honestly, men have no understanding do they, dear.' She threw another frown in Bill's direction before searching her bag for more tissues, but her supply had run out.

Fortunately the café owner, who'd been watching the trio with interest, brought out a box from behind the till and both women watched helplessly as Alison sobbed her way through them.

Bill, still feigning interest in the now empty fat-ball, was aware he'd triggered the fresh outbreak of tears, but had sympathy for the fellow who'd gone back to London; how was he supposed to know she wanted to rear a family by the sea, if she never told him? But he softened when he saw how upset Alison was.

Twenty minutes later, Marge was starting to fuss and Bill was getting edgy.

Alison had managed to drink a cup of tea, but couldn't face anything to eat so Marge and Bill shared her scone between them. From the look on Bill's face, that had been the only positive part of the afternoon.

'Now, are you sure you'll be okay?' Marge hesitated in her preparations to leave.

Feeling her throat tighten against yet another onslaught of tears, Alison was determined not to break down again. They'd been very kind, but were anxious to leave and she wanted to be on her own now.

'Yes, I'll be fine,' she promised, trying to focus on something that wouldn't set her off again.

'And make sure you get in touch with Richard for a good heart-to-heart.' Marge gave Alison's arm a squeeze as she turned to go.

'Yes, I'll do that.' Alison knew she wouldn't. 'And, thank you so much for stopping to help … oh, and thanks also for the tea. Please, don't let me keep you any longer.'

At last, Marge picked up her huge bag, gave a wave to the café owner and walked out of the door with Bill following closely, ready to block a retreat, should that be necessary.

Alison waved them off with a bright smile and, a minute or two later, got up to leave just before tears started to roll down her cheeks again. Through the corner of her eye, she caught the café owner's sympathetic look as she walked past. Fancy going into meltdown in front of total strangers; what must they have thought of her? Thank goodness she'd distracted Marge's attention away from exchanging phone numbers. They were a nice couple, but she knew she'd never want to meet them again.

It was late evening when Alison got back to her parents' house. Feeling utterly drained, she climbed the stairs to bed, relieved that the one good thing to come out of the day was that she'd made a clear decision on where to go from here.

CHAPTER 9

When Martin woke, he stretched his limbs luxuriously. The day before had been like a dream and a nightmare rolled into one.

He tried to concentrate on the dream aspects: an unexpected morning spent with Alison; their boat trip round the headland; fish and chips on the beach. But his mind kept going back to the nightmare moments: Richard turning up; his startling accusation; finding out he'd been rescued. That had been the worst part, but surely there was nothing to worry about now he'd withdrawn charges and gone home.

Martin frowned. His tendency to engage in worst-case scenarios meant he wasn't convinced. Also, he'd been disappointed when Alison said she didn't want to meet up today, especially as she'd been so touchy-feely yesterday. But, at least he had her new mobile number so would be able to keep in touch when she returned to London.

He was just drifting back to sleep when the phone rang and he heard his mother answer it. A moment later, she called up the stairs.

'Martin... it's for you.'

Martin flung back the duvet and picked up

the extension. 'Hello, Alison?'

'Is that Martin Landon?'

The voice was female, but it wasn't Alison. 'Yes.'

'Oh good,' said the woman. 'My name's Sandy and I'm phoning from "The Gazette." We heard about the accident at sea yesterday and wondered if you would give us an interview.

'We gather a friend of yours nearly died, but he's left the hotel where he was staying and we've not been able to contact him. Perhaps you could give us his number so we can talk to him as well?'

She paused, and when Martin didn't respond, continued: 'we've spoken to the lifeguard who rescued your friend and he said he was okay, but had said some rather strange things. He thought it was probably due to a head injury?'

She paused again. There was still no reply. She pressed on. 'Could we meet up? Perhaps if I came to see you ... or maybe we could get together on the sea front where your friend was brought in so we can take some pictures?'

This time Sandy waited several seconds. 'Are you still there?'

Martin drew in a deep breath before letting it out slowly and spoke in a voice that carried no trace of the pressure he was under. 'Unfortunately you've caught me at a bad time as I'm about to go away for a few days and have a train to catch; so I'm afraid I won't be able to meet you. In any case, there's very little I can add to what the lifeguard has already told you.'

'Oh, that is a shame,' said Sandy. 'It really would only take a few minutes of your time; and I could fit in with anywhere that suits you ... even at the station if that's of any help.'

Martin thought quickly. 'Well, I'm not leaving from Southcliffe,' he replied. 'I have a few things to do out of town first so will be going from the main line station.' Then he added, 'Jeez, is that the time? I'm running late so you must excuse me. I have to go now.'

'Oh ... perhaps when you get back, then...?'

At that point, he put the phone down so didn't hear Sandy pointing out how most people are only too happy to get their photo in the paper and it was a pity as it sounded like an interesting story.

Martin sat on the bed for a full minute while going through the implications of the call. First of all, he would have to give his mother a summary of what had happened. He'd hoped to avoid that because she had a way of looking at him that gave the impression she could read every thought; however, if the local paper knew, it would only a matter of time before someone mentioned it and she would wonder why he'd not told her.

Secondly, having said he was going away, perhaps he should do just that and then he would not be contactable; after all, he rarely took his full quota of leave, and the garage was quiet at the moment, so it shouldn't be difficult to arrange a few more days off.

After he'd made the phone call to his work place, he threw some clothes into a bag and went downstairs to find his mother.

Barely half an hour after ending his conversation with Sandy, Martin dropped a bag onto the back seat of his car and set off in the morning sunshine.

At that moment he had no idea where he was heading or what he was going to do with the week's holiday he'd just arranged.

CHAPTER 10

Ruth's head rested against the pane as she watched her son walk to his car. It was funny how she could superimpose her reflection onto him in the sunlit window as he opened the back door to stow his luggage. Best not look too closely though ... the lines looked deep in this light.

What if she were to change her hairstyle; add highlights for a softer look and update her wardrobe? But, there'd be no point. Only Martin would see it ... and he wouldn't notice if she were wearing a bin bag.

Ruth sighed. Maybe, she should have gone to university all those years ago; her parents had thought so and she'd got the grades. Why work in the wages department of a sausage factory when you could get a degree, they'd said? And, really there was no arguing with that ... except all she'd wanted then was go out and earn money.

Matthew had come into the office on her very first day. Some cock up with his pay slip, he'd said, and his butcher's overalls had been covered in blood from the killing line. Strange how he'd never noticed the smell ... even though it got everywhere ... Hair ... Clothes ... Ugh! His father had been the same only he...

Ruth shuddered.

Dad drinks because if he'd got the carpet mended when Mum asked, she wouldn't have fallen downstairs and broken her neck. That's how Matthew had described it ... all so matter-of-factly ... and just a few days after they'd started dating.

Perhaps she should have ended the relationship then ... What was it Grandma used to say? ... Something about apples and trees ... Ruth grimaced. Like father, like son, more like.

Martin was getting into his car now and Ruth inhaled sharply when she saw how like his father he looked. She gave a wave as he drove off, but he didn't respond so she went to the kitchen to put the kettle on.

It was the inheritance that changed everything ... My god, how they'd celebrated ... house by the sea, car and money ... all left by a distant cousin with no close relatives. It should have been a new beginning for them.

Matthew's eyes had lit up when he saw the house. Why don't we leave London and live here, he'd said. It'll be great for bringing up a family. He'd grabbed her hands and swung her round. But it had been a bad idea because, soon after they moved, he'd started going on about missing his job; although, it was really the social life he'd been hankering for ... which was why he'd spent so much time in the 'Southcliffe Arms' ... and that had led to him being offered the barman's job.

Maybe, if Martin had come along sooner? Ruth made herself a cup of tea and went back to the front room, where she chose a chair out of the sun. Dunking a biscuit, she flinched as she remembered the investigations they'd put themselves through.

Everything had come back normal so what *had* the problem been? Certainly it wasn't for the want of trying!

Get some part time work. It'll take your mind off it. That was always Matthew's answer, but, what did he know about the constant longing - day in, day out?

Still, the flower arranging job had been great ... a lifesaver really ... and he'd only seen the ad in the window because he'd taken to walking home ... How scared he'd been that evening when he nearly got caught. Just under the limit the officer had said and he knew he was a marked man after that.

The florist had been lovely. You've got a delicate touch and an eye for colour that can't be taught, she'd said and Matthew had been right. It did help.

Ruth sipped her tea, not wanting to think about the next part of her life but unable to stem the memories. Why did her parents move to Provence? We'll be back to visit, Mum had promised ... but they never came and rarely phoned ...

and of course she and Matthew were never invited over. She'd asked why, once. Could have done better for yourself, Dad had muttered so she never mentioned it again.

Then she fell pregnant ... just as they'd got used to the idea of no children. Perhaps it was the dreadful morning sickness that ruined it ... or the emergency caesarean ... and he wouldn't breastfeed, but loved the bottle ... just like his father!

Ruth gave a twisted smile.

Later, when Martin grew into a difficult toddler, she'd suffered depression and that, together with unremitting tiredness, meant she'd not had the energy to stop him biting and kicking other children. Unsurprisingly, parents stopped inviting her to their coffee mornings and loneliness became another constant.

She'd asked the doctor about it once; her fatigue and Martin's spitefulness; but he'd not been helpful. The boy will grow out of it and as for you, it's probably post-natal depression. That was all he'd said; in those days you just had to get on with it; but the weariness had clung to her like fog on a winter's day.

Ruth pulled a tissue from the box as another memory surfaced. That poor butterfly ... beautiful wings just torn off. She shivered. Why hadn't she stopped him? He was only five ... as his mother, she should have done something ...... but he'd looked so ... malevolent was only word to describe it.

Inevitably, Matthew lost his job as a barman. Redundancy, they'd called it, but she knew it was because of the booze. It had been the last straw for him and Ruth sometimes wondered if, in a rare sober moment, he'd decided to go in order to spare Martin the agonies he'd had to endure.

Looking back, she remembered how her husband's drinking got worse when Martin turned four ... the same age Matthew had been when his mother died ... and from then on they never knew what sort of mood he'd be in when he got home.

The day he left them was as clear in her mind as if it were yesterday. Even now she could hardly bear to think about what she'd nearly done and it had certainly been too much for Matthew because he'd strode off with scarcely a backward glance and never come back.

Quickly, she fast-forwarded to a time when Martin, by then at the Comprehensive, had got friendly with a classmate who also loved cars. For a brief period, he'd behaved like a normal teenager and then Tim stopped coming round.

Martin had said something about not wanting to hang out with him anymore, but Ruth pieced together the real story when she stood behind two women in a supermarket queue and overheard their conversation.

'It was awful. The poor lad couldn't have stood a chance,' the first woman was loading shopping onto the conveyor. 'He was on his way home from school and got pushed under a car. It seems there was a crowd of boys and one fell against him, sending him into the road ... Too many around to be sure which one, but with kids today you never really know, do you?'

'You don't think it was deliberate, do you?' Her companion's eyes widened as she added her own shopping to the moving belt.

The first woman shrugged. 'All I know is, Tim's lucky to be alive; it looks like he'll recover although he'll be in hospital for a while.

'Gracie was very upset as she and Tim have been getting close recently. Before that, I think he was friendly with another lad, but Tim dropped him once he met my Grace.'

That was when Ruth had known for certain her son was dangerous and a year or so later he'd got to know Alison.

They'd met by chance during the summer holidays, when both went for a daily swim and, as with Tim, Martin had been more settled; especially when they started going out together. But it ended when she went to university.

So tetchy he'd been around that time ... bitten her head off every time she opened her mouth. Eventually, he'd thrown all his energies into the garage, where he'd started as an apprentice, and that seemed to bring relief... until he discovered Alison had got engaged after she graduated.

Nibbling at a ragged fingernail, Ruth remembered how Martin moped in his room for days on end and there'd been nothing she could say or do to get through to him.

Then, shortly before Alison was due to get married, the fiancé had died in an accident and she'd headed off to London as soon as the funeral was over. But, at least Martin had nothing to do with that incident. He hadn't known the fiancé ... never even met him he'd said when she'd asked.

Ruth climbed rickety stairs to the attic, which she'd turned into a studio. Perhaps a spot of painting would take her mind off all this stuff she'd been dredging up.

'Never even met him?' That sounded familiar ... Oh yes, Martin said he'd 'never even met' the man in the boating accident until the day before ... so, why would he go out on the sea with someone he didn't know?

There was something else as well; the way he'd been acting since he got home last night ... Jumpy, but trying to cover it up.

Ruth concentrated on the detail of the flower she was painting while trying to quieten her troubled thoughts.

She'd have been even more worried if she'd

known Alison was back in town. But Martin had left that part out of his boating accident story.

CHAPTER 11

Once Martin had left the seaside town behind him, he started to relax. He'd given his mother a brief summary of how he'd helped someone in difficulties take a hire boat back to the Marina yesterday... and how the guy had fallen in the sea and nearly drowned.   Then, he'd gone on to explain that he was going camping and would be back in a week or so.

When he warned that "The Gazette" may get in touch again, she'd not said anything, but he knew from her expression she was suspicious. Annoyed that he'd had to tell her, he hoped yesterday's incident would be forgotten by the time he returned to Southcliffe.

Martin didn't have a plan when he set out but, as he drove, he realised he was following the London signs. With the motorway running freely, he allowed his thoughts to drift while speeding along in the outside lane.

Exactly why had Alison ended their relationship? She'd started to cool off just after her eighteenth birthday and the necklace he bought her had obviously been a mistake, even though he'd gone to a lot of trouble to get two good photos to put inside the silver heart that opened on a hinge.

Oh Martin, it's beautiful, she'd said. Thank you so much. But she didn't put it on. I won't wear it now because it won't fit over my polo jumper, had been the explanation and he never saw it again.

The next sign that things weren't right was when they went to the wedding of one of Alison's friends. The bride had been drinking and was teetering about in ridiculously high-heels, being over familiar with everyone. By the time she reached their table she could barely stand and draped an arm round each of them to prop herself up.

'Well, look at you two love birds,' she'd slurred and then giggled flirtatiously at Martin. 'Alison,' she went on, 'I really don't understand what's making you hesitate. He's gorgeous.'

She'd planted a wet kiss on both their cheeks and sniggered again while Martin, not used to such candour, had blushed furiously. The bride had hiccupped before staggering away, leaving Alison stony faced and Martin embarrassed. He'd been tempted to ask if she really was unsure about him - and if so, why - but something about the set of her jaw told him he wouldn't like the answer.

Martin scowled and tightened his grip on the wheel, recognising now what he'd failed to see then. Trying so hard to hold on to her had made her wary and the more he pushed, the more she backed off … until the day she told him outright it was over.

It had been a couple of weeks before she was due to go to uni and they'd been eating ice cream down on the sea front. Alison had stopped to lean over the wall and was gazing across the waves.

'I've been thinking,' she'd said. 'I'll be away for three years so it's really not fair to make you wait all that time … I mean, I don't want you to feel you can't date other girls while I'm gone.'

'I don't want to date other girls.' Martin had felt his stomach contract as she continued to avoid eye contact. 'It's you I want; no one else.'

'But, I'm going to be miles away. We'll never see each other.'

'Then I'll wait.' With hands thrust deep into his pockets, Martin tried to conceal the growing desperation.

'But I don't want you to wait,' she'd argued, voice sharpening as she walked on a bit further. 'I want to be free to make other friends and I can't do that if I'm tied to our relationship. Don't you see? This is a new beginning for me and I want to make the most of it. I'm sorry Martin, but I can't do that while I'm still going out with you.'

'But Alison-'

'-No! I've made up my mind.' She'd turned to face him and her eyes had been hard. 'I've really enjoyed our time together, but now I must move on. You'll find someone else - I know you will.' She'd moved forward to kiss his cheek. 'Good luck and thank you for everything.'

'But, you're not going yet,' Martin had grabbed her wrist as she turned away, 'why can't we see each other until you leave?'

'Martin, please...'

There'd been fear in her eyes and people were starting to look as he hung on tighter.

'You're hurting me ... Please let go.'

For a moment they'd stood, eyes locked.

'Martin! Let go of my arm ... now!' Alison had pulled away and taken a step back, rubbing her wrist. 'It's only a couple of weeks before I leave and I've got loads to do. It's time to make a clean break.'

'Will I see you in the holidays?'

'No, that's not a good idea.' She'd spoken more gently then. 'I don't want any commitment. It's been fun and I hope we can still be friends.'

With that, she'd turned and walked out of his life.

Still be friends. Martin sneered as he squeezed even harder on the steering wheel. That was a laugh. He'd only seen her once since then and that was at Paul's funeral.

Martin thought back to the previous morning when they'd sat on the beach together. He hadn't thought about Alison's first fiancé for a long time and it had been strange listening to her describe everything in such detail.

On hearing Paul had died after the accident, he'd found out the funeral arrangements immediately so he could be there. He'd wanted to sit with her during the service, but Fay and David had taken up those positions - one on each side - and at least one of them was with her most of that day.

He did manage a brief word while her parents were talking to Paul's mother and had thought she looked beautiful despite, or maybe because she was dressed entirely in black. The blonde hair, pulled back in a severe bun, had highlighted her pale face with its vivid blue eyes and it was all he could do to stop himself pulling her into his arms there and then.

'What are you going to do now?' he'd asked.

'I'm still going to London,' she'd replied. 'Dad's helping me move into a bed-sit next week.'

Having expected her to say she would stay in Southcliffe, Martin had been too surprised to respond when Alison added: 'Well, the job's waiting for me and I'm sure it's what Paul would have wanted ... you must excuse me Martin, I need to talk to Paul's mum. She's on her own.'

Alison had moved away - not to go over to Paul's mother, who'd just been approached by another mourner, but to rejoin her parents. He'd not set eyes on her again until she appeared in front of him on the beach a couple of days ago.

Martin's car, always in tip-top condition, was eating up the miles as he realised it was Alison's present fiancé who occupied his thoughts now. He pressed hard on the accelerator, thinking back to what Richard had said just twenty-four hours earlier and knew it was why he was making for London; he'd never rest until he'd settled that score.

Having been to the capital a few times, he decided not to drive into the city; instead he headed for Watford, which was less than an hour away by train.

Later that day, after taking a room in a budget hotel, he phoned a campsite a few miles along the coast from Southcliffe and booked a reservation for the following week. He wouldn't be able to track Richard down until after the weekend so that evening he set out to observe the lively nightlife of Watford as a way of killing time.

***

On Monday, Martin joined the rush hour commute and caught a train to the city, but it took until the following afternoon to locate Richard's place of work.

From there it had been simple and, once the deed was done, he drove to the campsite, arriving in the early hours of Wednesday when he parked in a residential road close by and dozed until daybreak. Later, he found a space in the middle of the car park and hoped no one would notice he'd only just arrived.

Dotted around were posters advertising the annual Southcliffe festival, due to start at the weekend, and he breathed a sigh of relief as it was highly unlikely that Sandy from "The Gazette" would have any further interest in last week's 'accident at sea' with all that going on.

Next week, he would go back to work and life would return to normal. At least that was the plan.

CHAPTER 12

Alison woke late on Sunday morning. She'd been exhausted after her walk the previous day so her parents left her to sleep in and it was eleven o'clock before she ventured downstairs in her dressing gown.

'Hello, love,' Fay was wiping her hands on a tea towel. 'I'm just about to do late breakfast. Would you like some?'

Realising she was very hungry, Alison nodded and went to sit opposite her father who was checking e-mails at the table. The kitchen hadn't changed in years and she was able to recapture the cosiness of her childhood when she saw how Fay still cooked in the same haphazard way, going from the fridge for eggs, to the cupboard for a frying pan then back to the fridge for bacon.

Alison smiled as Fay crossed the room yet again for plates. 'Why didn't you get everything out of the fridge before going to the cupboard? You must walk miles each time you cook a meal.'

David switched off his iPad and spoke in a mock stern voice. 'You leave her alone or she'll go on strike and we won't get any breakfast.'

'That's right.' Fay waved the butter knife at her daughter. 'You listen to what your father says. I'm multi-tasking.'

David and Alison burst out laughing.

'Oh, is that what it's called,' said David. 'I thought it was just being disorganised.' He ducked as Fay hurled the tea towel at him and Alison laughed, knowing these pretend fights were a symbol of her parents' strong relationship.

Familiar with the story of their romance, and how her father had proposed to his wife-to-be on her eighteenth birthday, she also knew that after twenty-seven years of marriage, her mother still considered him to be the perfect husband ... despite a few foibles, she would add, brows arched over twinkling eyes.

'Shall I lay the table?' Alison picked up the tea towel as she went to get the mats.

'Thank you, yes please.' Fay aimed a cuff at David as she passed. 'At least Alison offered some help.'

David grunted and picked up a supplement from the Sunday paper to retreat behind.

'Would you like to tell us about Friday, love? ... Something must have happened to make you change your mind about marrying Richard ... unless of course you've changed it back again ... Have you?'

Alison hid a smile. The casual attitude was never going to disguise her mother's curiosity and, over breakfast, she gave her parents a pared down version of everything that had happened since they arrived in Southcliffe. She was buttering toast when she told them about bumping into Martin so missed the anxious glances that crossed the table between them.

Then, after glossing over the hotel lunchtime conversation ... 'Richard was determined to carry on working so I told him I was going to meet up with Martin again,' ... she was also vague about the boat trip ... 'he decided to join us after all and hired a boat to follow; but, fell in the sea and had to be rescued.'

Lastly, she upgraded the frosty exchange between her and Richard in A&E to a full blown row and explained how her now ex-fiancé had caught the train back to London in a fit of temper.

'Then, Martin and I got fish and chips and ate it on the beach.' Alison feigned nonchalance as she finished her story, adding, 'It was a beautiful evening and it just felt so nice to be home again ... it still does.'

'Well,' said her father, 'it's been quite a weekend. Have you thought about what to do now? I suppose you'll be moving out of Richard's flat?'

Alison got up to clear away the breakfast things. 'Yes, I've been thinking about that. I can't go back ... well, not yet anyway ... could I stay here a bit longer? Then perhaps I can collect my things one day during the week while Richard's at work.'

'You can stay as long as you like, but you'll have to face him some time,' Fay took the plates from Alison and started to load the dishwasher. 'Does he know you're breaking off the engagement?'

Alison sighed. 'Not exactly, but, he won't be surprised. He knows I can't stand the way he runs out when things get tough. And he must have noticed how different we both were away from Docklands.'

'You'll need to find somewhere else to live if you're going to stay in London ... but, of course, moving back here is another option?' David added hopefully.

Alison reached for her father's hand and squeezed it. 'Thanks Dad, but I'm not going to walk away from my job. I've decided to look for somewhere to rent as I'm earning enough now to afford it; and I don't think I could go back to bed-sit land ... not after the luxury of Richard's apartment.

'I'll look for flats online and then make appointments to view them later in the week. I'll also ring work and book some leave. It's not like I do it often and I need to clear my head.'

'I've got a free day on Wednesday,' offered David. 'If you like I could go with you to collect your things.'

'Oh Dad,' Alison's face lit up, 'that would be

brilliant. I don't have a lot of stuff; only clothes and a few odds and ends; I might even be able to do it in one trip.'

'Well,' her father smiled disbelievingly, 'if I drive up in my car, I can take some things if necessary. Then you should only need to go in once.'

CHAPTER 13

On Wednesday morning, Alison and David set off in separate cars. The Dockland complex had both residential and visitors parking facilities so they arranged to meet in the courtyard around one thirty.

Alison left before her father as she had a couple of viewing appointments, but when she drew up outside the first property, it looked so dreadful she didn't even bother to park; however the next one, advertised privately, was better.

While the landlord was showing her round, it dawned on Alison just how spoiled she'd been while living with Richard. He employed a cleaner to come once a week so everywhere was immaculate and, although she'd financed the weekly shop, he'd taken no other money from her.

Here, the furnishings were old so it would always look shabby in comparison. Also, Alison would have to organise her time better. Travel would add two hours to her working day and, despite the low rent, she would have to watch her spending, which would be a pain, having got used to buying whatever she wanted without thinking too much about the cost.

On the plus side, there was a tube station a few minutes away so Alison decided to take the flat. She wouldn't stay long, but it would do as a stopgap while she worked out her long-term plans.

The elderly landlord, who lived with his wife on the ground floor, told her his name was Reg and explained how they'd been renting out the upstairs of their family home to top up their pension.

'Come down and meet Winnie,' he said, clearly delighted with his new tenant.

'Winnie also beamed when she saw Alison, 'Sit down, love and I'll make us a cup of tea. We'll have it in the garden.'

Sipping her tea in the shade of a cherry tree, Alison asked when she could move in. 'I suppose today is out of the question?' she ventured.

The couple looked at each other and Reg shrugged. 'Don't see why not, do you Win?'

Winnie shook her head vigorously. 'No, I don't see why not either, but what about your things?'

'Oh, I'm collecting them from my old flat, later. My father's helping me and we would be back in time not to disturb your evening.'

'Perfect.' Winnie clasped her hands and exchanged a smile of relief with Reg.'

'And the deposit and rent? Would it be okay to pay online?'

'Yes, online is fine,' Reg's smile faded. 'I know it's a lot to shell out up front, but we've had a couple of bad experiences with tenants ... not that we're anticipating any problems with you,' he added hastily. 'And it's what an agent would ask-'

'-it's fine Reg, really. It's what I was expecting.'

'Phew,' said Reg, wiping his forehead with the back of his hand. 'I'm glad we've sorted that out.'

Winnie smiled and patted his arm. 'We're not very good at this,' she confided.

Alison smiled back and pushed away thoughts of what she was giving up. But, there was no way she would go back to Richard now and she was grateful not to have to jump through all the referencing hoops an agency would have insisted on.

***

There'd been tears in Fay's eyes when Alison left that morning; but, she soon recovered ... it was always easier once her daughter had actually gone.

Earlier, she'd put a few bits and pieces in a bag for David to hand over when he met up with her. 'Alison would have told me not to fuss if I'd given them to her,' she'd said, 'but she may be very glad to see some of those things if she finds somewhere to stay today, so make sure she takes them ... and don't take no for an answer.'

David had chuckled. 'I'll try, but you know what Alison's like,' he'd replied, giving her a kiss.

'Yes I do, but leave them anyway ... and drive carefully.'

'Bye love,' David had kissed his wife again, 'and, don't wait up tonight ... I may be late back.'

The house seemed very empty once they'd both left and Fay decided to take her mind off the quietness by tackling a cupboard she'd been meaning to turn out for ages. There were all sorts of things in there, most of which belonged to Alison, so she would put them in a box to be sorted next time she visited.

Soon, Fay was discovering things that hadn't seen the light of day for months ... and in some cases, years.

After skimming through a packet of photos, most of which were of Alison as a little girl, she took out a large brown envelope and was intrigued to find a small box inside, together with a photograph. The picture was of Martin when he was about seventeen and the box contained a silver heart with a small catch which, when opened, revealed images of both of them. An inscription on the back read:

'*To Alison, love Martin x.*'

Fay sat back on her heels and looked from necklace to photograph, wondering why she felt so uneasy. Then she realised it was because she'd never seen these things before ... which meant Alison had never shown them to her. Also she'd not realised the relationship between her daughter and Martin had been serious enough for presents of this nature.

Surely Martin didn't have anything to do with Alison breaking off her engagement? Fay recalled the glances she and David had exchanged on Sunday when Alison mentioned his name. Then Martin and I had fish and chips on the beach, she'd said.

The more she thought about it, the more it made sense.

Oh dear, she sighed. I thought that was all finished years ago.

CHAPTER 14

Alison's heart thumped uncomfortably as she pulled into the visitor's parking area. It was approaching one thirty and glancing across the Docklands courtyard, she saw that Richard's bay had been coned off. That won't please him, she thought as she reversed into a space. I wonder where he's put his 'baby.'

She waved to her father who had just parked opposite and, as they walked towards the flat, David whistled through his teeth. 'This must set Richard back a bit.'

'Yes, I suppose it must.' Alison opened the door and wondered how much Richard paid each month. Up until this morning, she'd never really thought about it but, judging from the more modest flats she'd been checking out recently, she guessed it must cost a fortune.

Inside, everything was gleaming as usual and she calculated she could be away in twenty minutes if she put her mind to it.

'Wait here Dad, it's a beautiful view.' She pointed to a spacious seating area overlooking the river and thought of her own new outlook; a narrow road packed on either side with parked cars.

Sinking into a squishy leather sofa, David looked the epitome of an old fashioned schoolteacher, down to the well-worn trousers and checked jacket.

Now in his late forties, he retained boyish good looks and had the happy knack of being popular with his pupils whilst still maintaining discipline. Most of the girls had a crush on him and the boys wanted to be liked by him. He was also well thought of by other staff, but David appeared oblivious and that was part of his charm. Still head over heels in love with his wife, he was aware that many of his colleagues envied their relationship.

Fay was bound to cross examine him later about colour schemes and furnishings so after a few minutes he got up to take a slow walk round the flat, trying to commit it to memory and taking the odd photo to keep her happy.

The bathroom was fantastic with a huge old-fashioned bathtub, complete with lion claw feet, in the middle of the room. There were 'his' and 'her' hand basins and a big picture window that went down to the floor. David reckoned you'd get stunning views when lying in the bath, with Canary Wharf framed in the centre. Fay would love that. He chuckled as he imagined her in one of her 'bath bomb' explosions, looking out over the city.

The kitchen was also fitted out in chrome

and white, which was too clinical for David's liking. Yes, it may have all the latest gadgets, but some were so pristine, they looked like they'd only just been taken out of their boxes.

How many would justify their hefty price, he wondered? With the exception of a coffee machine and juicer, which had clearly been used that morning, he was only able to identify the bread maker, yogurt/soft cheese maker and hand held milk frother from the labels still attached. He was also mystified by the 'boiled egg cracker and topper?' Wouldn't a sharp tap with a teaspoon be just as efficient?

Back in the spacious lounge, a lack of clutter added to the 'show flat' impression and he'd been surprised by how few of Alison's possessions were on display. She enjoyed having knickknacks around and the only ornaments here were two large dragons that stood guard over Richard's display of top-of-the-range model cars. A nod to Harry Potter, David wouldn't wonder; he could imagine Richard being into that genre when he was younger.

Despite being in an idyllic setting, the apartment depressed David and he was glad when half an hour later, Alison stood in the hallway with three cases, a big bag of toiletries and a couple of sacks, filled with shoes. Other items included a table lamp and the throw they'd given her when she first came to London.

Seeing her father's eyebrows shoot up when

he saw the 'odds and ends' she'd mentioned last weekend, Alison said, 'I've left everything that Richard gave me. Otherwise there'd be twice as much!'

'Well, thank goodness for that.' David was sizing up the luggage and wondering how he could fit it into both cars. 'Are you sure that's everything?'

'Yes, I think so.' Alison placed an envelope on the table, which he guessed contained her engagement ring. 'If you start taking it down to the cars, I'll just have one more look round.'

'Well, try not to find anything else. We'll have enough trouble as it is doing it all in one journey.'

David was an orderly man and took his time packing the cars to make best use of the space. He was just putting the last bag into the front seat of Alison's car when a taxi drew up alongside and his heart sank as he saw Richard get out. At the same time, Alison had left the flat and was walking towards them while checking her phone. There was no time to warn her and, when they saw each other, both stopped and stared in amazement.

'What are you doing here?' Richard recovered first, moving between Alison and her father with his arms folded.

'I'm sorry, Richard,' Alison spoke quickly. 'Dad came with me to get my things. I've posted the keys through the letterbox and I'm afraid the engagement is off.'

David squirmed at his daughter's bluntness, but Richard met it head on, his voice acid with sarcasm.

'Am I supposed to be surprised? Seeing as how you've not bothered to get in touch since the weekend.'

'It would never have worked, Richard.' Alison's eyes shone behind unshed tears. 'We were fine while both of us were working, but away from here we had nothing in common ... You must have seen that?'

There was a pause and David held his breath, ready to step in if necessary. But Richard just nodded and shrugged.

'Yes, you're probably right ... still friends though?'

David covered a smile. Not many people could wrong foot his daughter. Although she was hiding it well, Alison would have expected Richard to put up a bit more of a fight and he wasn't surprised at her response.

'If you like ... but, I doubt we'll see much of each other as I'll be living too far away to meet up. Why don't we just say goodbye and move on?'

Richard hesitated before nodding again. 'Okay, if that's what you want.' He started to walk towards his flat.

'Why are you here, Richard?' Alison called after him. 'You never come home during the day.'

'No, and I wouldn't be here now except last night someone had a go at my car.'

'Really,' Alison's eyes widened. 'What happened?'

'All four tyres slashed and the bodywork keyed right round.' Richard scowled. 'That's what happened. Come and see.'

He led the way to a remote part of the car park and both Alison and David gasped when they saw the vandalised Porsche.

'How did that happen with all the security they've got here?' Alison walked slowly round the vehicle, her shocked gaze taking in scratches and gouges so deep that some had gone right through the metalwork. 'Is it on CCTV?'

'Well, that's the infuriating thing.' Richard stroked the bonnet of his spoiled car. 'When I got home last night, my usual parking space was coned off so I had to park here where it's not well lit. The security man checked the tape, but it was too dark to see anything.'

'Why didn't the alarm go off?' asked David.

Richard looked sheepish. 'It was very sensitive and needed adjusting,' he explained. 'I'd been meaning to get it done, but one evening the wind set it off three times so I just disabled it ... Then I forgot about it, which I know was stupid ... but it looks like I'll pay in spades now as I doubt the insurance will cover it.'

'But, who would do such a thing?' Alison

nudged a toe against one of the shredded tyres, causing another strip of rubber to fall away.

'You may well ask,' said Richard. 'I have my suspicions, but if I tell you, you'll say I'm paranoid.'

'Well, go on then; who do you think did it?'

'I believe it was Martin.'

Alison's face reddened as she stamped her foot and David was reminded of childhood tantrums in supermarkets.

'You're being ridiculous again,' she shouted. 'Why the hell would you think that?'

'Because I could have sworn Martin was in the next carriage of the train I came home in last night, that's why.'

David broke in before Alison could respond. 'But why would Martin, who you hardly know, do something like this?'

'For the same reason he tried to kill me last Friday. That is one very jealous guy, if you ask me.'

'I don't believe it,' snapped Alison, 'and I can prove it. I got this text from Martin, yesterday evening.' She scrolled down her phone and showed the message to Richard.

'hi al, hope u got back ok. spending a few days at the old camp site. been here since yesterday and staying til the weekend. it was gr8 2 c u again.'

'See, he couldn't have been here. He was

miles away.' She jabbed her finger on the date of the text and pushed the phone under Richard's nose.

'You can send a text message from anywhere,' replied Richard as he started to walk away. 'It doesn't mean a thing.'

'Well, I tell you what, then,' Alison yelled, 'I'll phone the campsite and prove it once and for all.'

'Oh, I wouldn't bother.' Richard's lip curled as he looked back over his shoulder. 'I've no doubt he's covered his tracks and it'll take more than a phone call to convince me it wasn't him.'

'Well, it'd be pointless trying then, wouldn't it?' Alison turned on her heel and stormed off to her car.

David, still trying to get his head round what had just been said, caught up with Richard and grabbed his arm. 'What do you mean, Martin tried to kill you?'

'It's true ... but, everyone thinks it was an accident when I fell in the sea at the weekend. Did Alison tell you about that?'

'A little; something about you going overboard when the boat went round the headland?'

'Hmm, that seems to be the general understanding. But, I'm sure that's not how it happened.' He frowned. 'The annoying thing is, I can't remember ... but, I have a gut feeling Martin was responsible.'

'Sounds a bit extreme?' Out of the corner of

his eye, David could see his daughter, drumming her fingers on the steering wheel. 'Alison said you'd only met him the day before. What possible motive could he have?'

'I told you; jealousy.' Richard was also watching Alison. 'They used to have a thing going and as soon as I saw him I knew he still fancied the pants off her.'

David's jaw dropped.

'Sorry David,' Richard clapped him on the shoulder. 'Too much information for a father I suppose, but I know I'm not wrong, even though Alison won't admit it.'

They both turned as a trailer backed into the courtyard.

'Ah, that must be from the garage. They've come to collect the car.' Richard signalled to the driver and held out his hand. 'It was nice to meet you, David ... and Fay, of course. You have a lovely daughter, but sadly she doesn't think I'm the right man for her. Take my advice. Don't let her get caught up with Martin again. He's not good news, believe me.'

David shook hands. 'Goodbye, Richard. I hope you get your car fixed.'

There was an impatient toot from Alison's car. 'Come on, Dad,' she shouted. 'I need to get back before the rush starts and it's over an hour's drive away.' She handed the address through the window when he came over. 'Do you want to follow me?'

'No,' said David. 'We might get separated and you can get there quicker if you don't have to worry about me. I'll use the sat nav your mother gave me.'

'Good idea. I'll see you there, then.'

Alison pulled out of the courtyard without a backward glance so she didn't see Richard watching until her car was out of sight.

CHAPTER 15

Driving away from Richard's flat, David followed instructions from the calm sat nav woman and chuckled as she recalculated when he made a wrong turning. There'd have been hell to pay had Fay been navigating.

When he arrived at the address late afternoon, the first thing he noticed was the lack of parking. This will wind Alison up he thought while reversing into a tight space thirty metres or so down the road. He started to unload, calculating it would take four trips to ferry Alison's things to the flat; and his daughter was already unpacking by the time he walked in with the first load.

'Hi Dad,' Alison greeted her father with a peck on the cheek. 'I'm afraid there's nothing here to offer in the way of refreshment. I'll have to go shopping as soon as we've brought everything in. Apparently there's a supermarket not far away.'

'I'll take you in my car,' offered David. 'Then you won't lose your space. We could also get something to eat as well.'

'Good idea,' said Alison and a couple of hours later they were sitting in a local Italian restaurant waiting for the main course to be served.

'How are you feeling?' asked David.

'Oh, I don't know,' Alison poured two glasses of water from the jug on the table. 'Seeing Richard again, I can't believe I ever wanted to marry him; although I am going to miss living in Docklands.' She gave her father a lop-sided grin.

'Yes, it's some flat,' agreed David. 'Even so, I think you've done the right thing. Richard's all right, but I agree with your mother, he's not the man for you. Sooo ... Do you have plans for the future ... or are they not for sharing?'

'They don't have to be a secret.' Alison smiled as she helped herself to garlic bread. 'And I am thinking of coming home again, but not to live with you and Mum ... Oh, Dad, that came out all wrong. It's just that I've got used to being independent and don't think it would be good for any of us if I moved back. You and Mum have your own lives-'

'-it's okay, love.' David squeezed her hand across the table. 'And you're quite right. You need your own space, but it would be nice to have you living close by again. Are you sure that's what you want, though? What about your job?'

'Well, I can't deny the money's nice, but coming home made me realise how quality of life is more important.'

'Meeting up with Martin wouldn't have had anything to do with it then?'

'No, of course not!' Alison's reply was a shade too quick as she glanced away. 'But, I've decided to check out local vacancies and should stand a good chance of getting a transfer, especially with my London experience.'

'You're going to stay in banking, then?'

'For now, I think.'

The food arrived and they gave it their full attention. Then, when they'd finished eating, Alison stifled a yawn and David looked at his watch. 'Well, we'd better be getting you back,' he said while signalling to the waiter. 'You must be tired and I have a long journey ahead.'

***

After dropping Alison off, David set the sat nav so he could follow it to the motorway. As he drove, he thought back to the extraordinary conversation he'd had with Richard earlier. The accusations had unsettled him more than he realised and he tried to remember what Martin was like when he was younger.

He'd gone to the Comp, but David couldn't recall having him in his class and frowned as he tried to think of anything that might distinguish him from all the other kids. There had been something ... and then he remembered Tim Burgess. The two had been inseparable for a while and staff had commented on how much more sociable Martin became once he started to hang around with Tim.

David gave his attention to a tricky right

turn onto the motorway and pulled the visor down against the setting sun. Picking up speed, he changed lanes to settle into the long journey home.

What happened to that friendship? Hadn't there'd been a girl involved ... Grace? ... Yes, Tim had started to go out with Grace ... and then there'd been an unpleasant incident.

He pulled out to overtake a lorry and, back in the middle lane, searched his memory for details. Tim had ended up under a car and there was talk that it hadn't been an accident.

David frowned again. Richard said his ducking in the sea hadn't been accidental. He said it was down to Martin, but surely that was in his imagination.

The sun sank lower and David reached for his sunglasses. Two near fatalities, several years apart, but was it possible they were linked?

What was it Richard said; something about Martin not being good news? He didn't seem the sort of man to make things up ... in any case, what would be the point? He'd accepted he wasn't right for Alison and in all honesty, didn't seem too concerned about the broken engagement. He was more upset about the Porsche.

And that was another thing. Why would Richard pretend he'd seen Martin on the train? And why would anyone want to damage such a lovely car?

David was aware that the alarm bells in his

head had just got louder. He really hoped Alison wouldn't take up with Martin again, but sighed as he suspected the main reason she'd decided to come home was to be near her old boyfriend.

***

Alison waved her father off then went back upstairs to her new flat and sank onto the faded chintz sofa. Glancing round, she couldn't help thinking about where she would have been, had she stayed with Richard.

Out on the balcony most likely, with a glass of chilled wine; she shook away the image. It was another lovely evening, but here she could only see a small patch of sunlight reflected onto the wall from a window across the road.

The kitchen faced west so at least that would be bright in the evenings; but her brow puckered when sunlight showed how everywhere was in need of what her mother would call 'a damn good clean.'

However, now all she wanted to do was sleep and, when she saw the towels and bedding her father had brought for her, she sent out a silent thank you to her mother. There was also a mattress cover, which Alison was particularly pleased to see.

Quickly, she made up the bed and cleaned her teeth in the tiny bathroom, which also boasted a layer of grime on all surfaces. But, she breathed a sigh of relief when she found the shower worked and was reasonably efficient.

Ten minutes later, with curtains drawn against the fading light, Alison climbed into bed and fell asleep almost immediately.

CHAPTER 16

Alison woke early and the empty hours stretched ahead. She'd have to find a way to fill them otherwise she'd go mad.

Just as yesterday David had calculated the number of trips he would need to make between car and flat, Alison estimated the amount of time it would take to make her new home habitable. If she got stuck in, she should have it done in a day ... and even if I haven't, I'll have had enough by then, she thought.

After scouring out a mug, she made tea, but gave toast a miss when she saw the ancient toaster and the state of the grill. Instead, determined to stay focussed, she filled a bucket with hot water, threw in disinfectant, all purpose cleaner and bleach before pulling on a pair of Marigolds.

Reg popped in while she was washing down the kitchen cupboards and was impressed. Previous tenants had done little or nothing in the flat and, despite an attempt to clean up before Alison arrived, he and his wife had been defeated by the enormity of the task.

'The carpets are filthy,' Alison, who had been appalled when she looked closely, waved a gloved hand at suspicious looking stains when she saw Reg watching.

Reg went pink and took out a hanky to polish his glasses. 'Yes, I'm sorry about that. If we'd known we'd be lucky enough to get someone like you we'd have got them cleaned. I'll look out a flyer that came through the door the other day. Winnie's bound to have stashed it away somewhere.'

Reg came back later with the carpet cleaner's details. 'Win suggested you take the curtains to the dry cleaners, as well,' he added. 'There's one in the grounds of the supermarket; I'll pay.'

'Thanks, I will,' said Alison, just as her stomach made a loud rumbling noise.

Reg chuckled. 'Sounds like you need to stop for something to eat,' he said, heading back to the stairs.

Alison checked the time on her phone and realised it was four hours since she'd skipped breakfast. A few minutes later, while devouring a quick sandwich, she looked round the kitchen and gave a satisfied nod.

It had scrubbed up okay and, having already tackled the bathroom, she knew she could easily get through the rest of the flat by the end of the day. If she took the curtains to the cleaners first - Reg had said to use their express service, adding that he would collect and re-hang them when they were ready - there would be nothing pressingly urgent left to do.

While finishing her coffee, Alison rang the carpet cleaners and arranged for them to come early the following morning. You're in luck, the man had said, we've just had a cancellation.

Switching off the call, she then gave serious thought to an idea that had been buzzing round in her head all morning. Why not join Martin at the campsite? He'd said he'd be staying 'til Sunday ... and she'd have to leave then to get back in time for work. But, that would still give them nearly two days together. Two nights as well thought Alison as a thrill ran through her.

Quickly, she took up her phone again and found Martin's number, pressing call before she could change her mind.

'Hello, Alison?' the voice sounded wary.

'Hi Martin, yes it's me.' Feeling ridiculously nervous, she added, 'How're you doing?'

'Fine ... are you phoning from work?'

'No, I've taken a few days off. I was wondering if you're still at the campsite ... and if I could come and spend the weekend with you?'

There was a long pause and Alison pictured him struggling to get his head round what he'd just heard.

'Y-yes, of course, you can,' he stammered at last. 'Um ... when were you thinking of coming?'

'Tomorrow afternoon, if that's okay. I'll send a text when I arrive; then perhaps you could meet me at reception.'

'Absolutely,' said Martin. 'It'll be great to see you.' He hesitated again. 'What about Richard?'

'Oh, I'll tell you when I get there. See you tomorrow, then?'

'Yes, see you tomorrow ... Bye.'

With her heart still fluttering from the sound of Martin's voice, Alison unhooked all the curtains and bundled them up while sneezing loudly into the cloud of dust she'd created.

Staggering with them down to the car, she realised it was almost a week since she'd met Martin on the beach. And she couldn't wait to see him again.

Next morning, Alison waited impatiently for the carpet cleaner to turn up, having packed ready to leave as soon as he arrived.

Reg had said to tell the man to see him downstairs when he'd finished so as soon as he knocked, Alison showed him what needed doing and left him to it.

She now had the whole weekend to look forward to and hadn't given a single thought to Richard since leaving Docklands the previous day.

CHAPTER 17

Richard frowned as he watched first Alison, then David, pull out of the courtyard. He should be feeling sad, but it was almost like watching two strangers drive away. In fact, he was enjoying an unexpected sense of freedom as he went to join the two men from the trailer who were standing by the Porsche and examining the damage.

'This joker really meant business, didn't he?' The driver's badge identified him as Joe.

'Why? What do you mean?' Richard felt his pulse quicken.

Joe's eyes narrowed as he squinted against the sun. 'Well, you can see how a lot of anger went into the tyre slashing. One long cut on each would have been enough, but look what he's done.' He bent down to point to the tyre that Alison had kicked; and which had now nearly fallen away from the wheel. 'The guy really laid into them. They're cut to ribbons and it must've taken quite a while to do this amount of damage.'

Richard looked more closely and clenched his fists at the thought of what he'd do if he ever got his hands on Martin.

'Then, there's the keying.' Joe had moved round to the boot. 'Whoever did it made sure every single part of the car was scraped.'

'What are you saying?'

'Well, if you ask me-'

'-not now, mate. He doesn't want to hear it.' The other man chipped in, turning to Richard as he added, 'Joe's doing a psychology course. Last night was all about anger and aggression and I've already heard the lecture on the way down.'

Joe laughed. 'But, it's interesting. And I've certainly learned a thing or two about human nature.'

'What were you going to say?' asked Richard.

Joe hesitated. 'Well … let's just say perhaps it's a good job it was your car he found and not you.'

Another shiver ran through Richard as he remembered his lucky escape at the weekend.

'Yes, that's as maybe,' Joe's mate was looking at his watch, 'but we've got to get back to the garage because there's another pick up to do after this one.'

Richard's heart was racing as he watched the two men load up and edge cautiously out of the courtyard. Until Joe's analysis, he hadn't even considered how the extent of damage might be significant and, opening the apartment door a minute or two later, he wondered if Alison had dished out the same kind of vengeance; but everything was as he'd left it, apart from the disappearance of her things.

After tipping the ring out of the envelope she'd left and reading the note; which said more or less the same as she'd said in the car park; he sighed. Already the flat felt empty without her presence.

Selecting an app on his phone, he ordered a taxi and went outside to wait in the shade. The more he thought about it, the more sure he was that Martin had been on the train yesterday. Alison was bound to have told him about the flat ... and probably mentioned what he did for a living to explain how he could afford it ... so he would have been reasonably easy to track down.

Martin also knew about the Porsche and would have seen him drive off if he'd followed him back from the station.

Why had his parking space been coned off? He must find out about that. It was too big a coincidence that his car was vandalised on the day he had to leave it somewhere less secure ... and also on the day he was sure Martin was in London.

CHAPTER 18

Martin switched his phone off and put it in his pocket. Did Alison really just invite herself down for the weekend? The thought that it might be to do with the way he looked never crossed his mind.

'Fit,' was how most girls would describe him because Martin was particular about his appearance. He paid a lot to keep his dark hair casually stylish and the brown eyes were deep-set and long lashed. Also, blessed with olive skin that bronzed easily and being out in all weathers, he always had a tan.

Then there was the collection of well fitting jeans, invariably teamed with a plain black or white T-shirt. Occasionally he added a checked shirt or fleece, but rarely felt the cold so seldom wore a sweater. If it rained, he would put on the leather jacket he bought in his teens that had weathered to fit the contours of his body like a second skin.

Trainers were his other weakness and he owned several pairs, discarding them immediately they became scruffy.

Martin never appeared to notice admiring glances and it was this, together with his detached manner that gave him an air of mystery. The only puzzle was that he never took advantage of it.

There'd been rumours he might be gay, but the reality was Martin paid little attention to anyone of either sex. He'd never looked to replace Alison and now his dream of getting her back was gaining substance, he grappled to understand why.

What qualities did he have to make him more attractive than a successful stockbroker with a Docklands flat and top-of-the-range sports car?

Martin thought back to Tuesday. Considering those were the only facts he had on Alison's new fiancé ... and that the Southcliffe police had referred to him as Mr Clancy ... it had not been too difficult to find Richard.

A few questions in the Stock Exchange - fortunately someone recognised the name - had narrowed the search to a tower block in the heart of the city; and, once he'd located it, he found a vantage place in the window of a café opposite where he watched for Richard to leave. Guessing he'd use the tube, Martin was glad he'd already bought a travel card for the journey in from Watford.

It was mid afternoon when Richard came out of the building, carrying a briefcase and talking hands free on a mobile, which hopefully would distract him from noticing he had company.

Part time workers! Martin had frowned with disapproval as he followed him to the station where an escalator took them down to a platform that was emptier than the streets had been. After briefly considering the possibility of another 'accident,' Martin decided there weren't enough people around to cover the deliberate push needed so, when the train arrived, he got into the adjacent carriage to follow him home.

At one point he thought his cover was blown when an inspector opened the end door of the coach to walk through the train and Richard appeared to stare right at him; but, when he got out at Canary Wharf, he didn't look back and, after a ten minute walk, turned into the courtyard of a block of apartments near the river.

Martin could almost smell the money and it was further proof of just how far Alison had come. However, having established where he lived, he wasn't sure what to do next. There would be CCTV here so he shouldn't hang around but, as he turned to leave, he saw Richard walking towards an immaculate red car parked in the front of the courtyard.

Of course! He'd forgotten the Porsche and turning his back to the road, pretended to adjust his trainer as Richard drove past.

Straightening up, once the car was out of sight, Martin nearly fell over one of four cones, tied together with orange tape in a rectangle that surrounded a section of damaged paving.

There was also a red 'danger' triangle to warn pedestrians of the hazard. The cordoned off area was about the same size as a parking bay and that's what gave Martin the idea to seal off Richard's space so he would have to park somewhere else.

It was a long shot; he might move the cones and park there anyway; but Martin didn't think so. The visitor's car park had a couple of free spaces under some trees where, as far as he could tell, there was only one camera and fewer lampposts. When he got back, Richard would probably put the car there, at least for one night.

Having no better ideas, Martin pulled up the hood of his fleece and moved the cones and triangle to Richard's bay before walking back to the station.

Later that day, after collecting his car, he would drive back; but the next part of his plan wouldn't be easy because Martin's love of cars matched Richard's. However, the very fact of knowing how much it would hurt, made him realise there was probably no better way to get revenge on such a petrol head.

Sadly for Richard, everything worked perfectly. Even Martin was shocked by the violence that went into his act of sabotage, having intended only to destroy all four tyres and leave it at that; but, when the alarm didn't go off, he'd grabbed a screwdriver and gouged every surface before heading back to his own car.

Serves him right, he'd thought as he sped away high on adrenaline and a sense of 'mission accomplished.'

The following morning, after arriving at the campsite, Martin had just finished setting up his tent when he called out to a group of people passing.

'Looks like it going to be hot again, doesn't it?'

'Yes ...hope it stays.' The young girl, who turned to reply, blushed under Martin's gaze.

'Well, it's been okay here since the weekend so no reason why it shouldn't.' Martin looked away when the girl hesitated as if about to come over; then waited anxiously until she continued on with her friends. Not exactly an alibi for yesterday, but hopefully she'd remember if anyone asked about him.

But, would Richard really think of Martin when he saw the damage? He'd been right about the lack of lighting and had carried out his act of destruction in near total darkness. It was unlikely a camera would pick up much detail and anyway, his hooded fleece would give the impression of a teenage vandal.

By Thursday afternoon, Martin had started to get bored. Then Alison called making the next few days sound much more promising.

CHAPTER 19

Alison pulled into the campsite on Friday afternoon to find Martin waiting just inside the gates. Her insides flipped as he walked over and she opened the door so he could ride with her to the car park.

'I didn't get a chance to tell you,' he said, sliding into the passenger seat, 'it's a very small tent and I've only got basic essentials here. We could find somewhere more comfortable if you prefer.'

'It'll be fine.' Alison's heart beat faster when she heard the words 'small tent'. 'It's just for two nights and the weather's still gorgeous so I'm sure we'll manage. I've only brought a sleeping bag and one small case.'

They carried Alison's gear to the tent and a quiver ran through her when she saw again how different Martin was to her ex fiancé. She tried to picture camping with Richard, but her imagination just wouldn't make that leap.

'Shall we swim? There's a good beach and the tide is in.'

'That'd be great.' Alison rummaged for her swimming things. 'I can't wait to wash away the London grime.'

Martin halted in the search for his own towel

and looked up. 'I thought you'd taken time off work … didn't you phone from your parents house?'

'Nope.' Wriggling into flip-flops, Alison scraped her hair into a ponytail. 'I only stayed a couple of days and then went back on Wednesday.'

'How was Richard?'

'Oh, I didn't go back to him … At least I didn't stay … I only went to pick up my stuff. I've rented a flat in Middlesex for now … And I've broken off the engagement if that's what you're wondering.'

'Because of last weekend?'

'Pretty much … although things began to go wrong once he'd met my parents.' Alison was trying to work out what was going on behind the mask of indifference as she headed towards the sea. 'It wasn't that they didn't like each other … more that Richard didn't fit into Southcliffe. He was missing the city even before we arrived.

'Last Saturday's fiasco was the pits and I think he knew that. He certainly didn't seem surprised when I told him it was over between us.'

As they slithered down a steep slope to the beach, Alison revelled in the warmth of the sea breeze. 'To be honest, Richard seemed more interested in his car,' she said, turning her face to the sun. 'Someone gave it a real going over and to say he wasn't happy, is putting it mildly. … You won't believe this, but he actually thinks it was you who did it.'

Alison had her eyes half shut against the glare so didn't see Martin's face drop as he fell behind.

'Me?' he said, taking long strides to catch up, 'Why me?'

'He thought he saw you in the train on Tuesday. I told him you were here, but he was having none of it.' She gave Martin a nudge, which knocked him off balance. 'He's taken a real dislike to you ... I wonder why.'

Martin ignored the irony. 'Knowing we used to go out together wouldn't have helped. He must have seen me as a threat.'

Alison frowned. 'I suppose so ... but we were teenagers and that was ages ago.'

Laying out the blanket, she realised how last time she'd done this she'd been someone else's fiancée. Then, Martin had behaved very properly.

So much had changed in just a few days and she was beginning to enjoy the freedom. She shouldn't jump straight into another relationship but Martin, having stripped off his T-shirt, was in good shape and drew glances from women of all ages.

She smiled as she pulled her own T-shirt over her head. It didn't have to be serious, and he was no longer obsessed with her, so she would see how the weekend went and take it from there.

They walked down to the shoreline and Alison reached for Martin's hand as they waded in. The water felt deliciously cool and she relaxed as the stress of the last few days melted away. Turning to Martin at the same time he turned to her, their faces were inches apart.

'Hello Martin,' she said.

'Hello Alison.'

Then they were in each other's arms and by the time they left the water, both were clear about the delights in store for the rest of the weekend.

***

The hours flew by and all too soon it was Sunday and time to leave.

'When will I see you again?' Martin was helping Alison to bring her things to the car.

'Soon...' She thought back to earlier when they'd clung to each other in the tent and she'd told him she was going to move back to Southcliffe.

'I think a local position may be coming up so I could be home in a matter of weeks.' She sighed as he kissed the back of her neck. 'Perhaps we could meet halfway at a hotel sometimes while we wait,' she added.

'I'd like that.' Martin lifted her case into the boot and turned to wrap her in a bear hug. 'Let's do it very soon.'

'Easy, Tiger,' Alison laughed as she freed herself and threw her bag onto the passenger seat. 'I'll be in touch, don't worry.'

He caught her in another embrace and kissed her hard. 'Come home quickly,' he said, huskily.

'I will.' Alison pulled away reluctantly and climbed into her car. She waved as she drove off and watched through the windscreen mirror until he was out of sight, her heart sinking at the thought of the shabby flat waiting for her.

A short while later when she turned onto the motorway, the sky was darkening. Soon rain began to fall in sheets and she was having difficulty seeing through the spray, even with the wipers on double speed.

Why was she rushing to get somewhere she didn't want to go? She pulled over to the inside lane and slowed down resolving to do everything she could to get back to Southcliffe as soon as possible.

Five miles on, a double line of red lights stretched ahead as far as she could see and she applied her own brakes to join the procession. She'd forgotten how Sunday traffic built up. What a miserable end to a great weekend.

With her foot switching automatically from brake to accelerator, she allowed her thoughts to drift back to the few precious hours she'd spent with Martin and her pulse quickened as she re-lived those intimate moments inside that ridiculously small tent. She smiled at the memory. Then, an impatient toot from the car behind brought her back to reality and she moved forward another few metres while waving an apology.

It was late evening when Alison finally let herself into the flat and was met by the aroma of newly cleaned carpets, mixed with a chemical smell of dry cleaning fluid that clung to the curtains Reg had re-hung.

Switching on the lights, she looked round and realised her living conditions had improved considerately since she moved in a few days earlier. The flat would do in the short term and tomorrow, she'd check out the bank vacancy site. Then, once back in Southcliffe, she'd look more carefully into her long-term plans, which would now include Martin.

Alison drew the curtains to shut out the dreary view and got ready for bed. After setting the alarm for six thirty – no more lie-ins - she fell asleep quickly and dreamt of the passionate nights she and Martin had spent together. Already she was thinking about their next meeting ... which she'd make certain would happen soon.

***

When Alison's car disappeared from view, Martin walked slowly to the tent to pack up his own things before driving back to Southcliffe. He was in no hurry and would leave it as late as possible before setting off.

He would have to tell his mother about Alison now ... but not tonight. That way he could keep her to himself a bit longer.

The sun went in and a breeze sprang up, chilling the air. The heat wave was at an end, but what a weekend it had been. Martin knew he would never forget it.

As he left the campsite, the first fat drops of rain started to fall, but Martin didn't care. Richard was gone and Alison was back in his life. He could hardly believe it.

By the time he arrived home, his mother had gone to bed and he left for work the following morning before she was up. She'd left no messages so he assumed "The Gazette" had lost interest.

He really meant to tell her about Alison, but the moment never seemed right.

CHAPTER 20

While Alison was on her way to meet Martin at the campsite, Fay was nearing the end of her shift at a charity shop where she worked half a day every Friday. David had been amused when she volunteered. I thought they were staffed by the blue rinse brigade, he'd smiled and she'd chided him for being 'so last century.'

Now in her mid-forties, Fay would easily pass for a younger woman, holding the years at bay by sticking to a strict skincare regime and keeping her makeup simple. As she brushed her hair, highlighted and styled in the same shoulder-length bob she'd worn since teenage years, she certainly didn't fit the image her husband had conjured up. And, when she handed the till key to another stylish woman, her replacement also kicked David's stereotype into touch.

One of the few to make good use of her gym subscription, Fay was dedicated to staying fit and had just started out on the forty minute walk home when she bumped into Ruth, coming from the opposite direction.

They usually said hello when passing, but today Fay stopped and barred the way before adding, 'Alison and Martin seem to be hitting it off again, don't they?' Her eyes narrowed as Ruth tried to disguise the gasp of shock behind a cough. 'Didn't Martin tell you they met up last weekend when she was down for a visit?'

'Oh ... yes, of course ... it slipped my mind. My memory's not so good these days.'

'Well, Alison's gone back to London now, but she's looking to move here again. I think she's had her fill of the capital and misses being by the sea.

'She's broken off her engagement to a stockbroker because she knew he'd never move from the city. Richard was the chap who nearly drowned. I think Martin was with him at the time, wasn't he?'

When Ruth made no comment, Fay continued:

'Poor Richard, it really wasn't his week. Apparently, someone vandalised his lovely car on Tuesday night ... outside his flat in Docklands. David saw it when he went up with Alison to collect her things. Every tyre ripped to shreds and the bodywork scratched. Richard was distraught...'

Trapped on the narrow footpath by this unexpected encounter, Ruth felt the blood drain from her face. There'd been an emphasis on the word 'someone' and she knew Alison's mother was watching her closely.

'That must have been awful for him … And I'm sorry the engagement didn't work out, but I suppose it's a good thing Alison found out sooner rather than later,' she stammered.

'Yes, well, your Martin could have had something to do with that.' Fay's voice had hardened, 'They had supper together on the beach after Richard went home last weekend.'

'Oh … I didn't know that.'

Too shocked to even try and conceal her surprise this time, Ruth's instincts were on high alert. One tragedy had been averted, but how long before something really bad happened? It would be fine as long as Alison stayed with Martin. But she'd got bored last time … and that was before she'd had a taste of London life.

Fay stepped to one side, allowing Ruth to hurry off and they went separate ways, each with their own worrying thoughts.

CHAPTER 21

Summer passed and Alison settled into her new life better than she'd expected. The local post she'd been planning to apply for was withdrawn and no further vacancies had come up, but she was beginning to enjoy London again so the urge to go home lessened.

Her landlords were also pleased with their latest tenant as it meant they no longer had to worry about what was going on upstairs. Winnie, always up for a chat, loved to visit and usually came with offerings of cakes or puddings when she'd been baking.

As time went on, she was feeding Alison practically every day, either taking something up or, more often, inviting her to eat with them downstairs and, when Alison offered to pay, Winnie wouldn't hear of it. I have to cook for Reg and me she would say and an extra portion makes hardly any difference. It seems silly to use two cookers and besides, we love having you pop down, don't we Reg?'

Her husband, usually deep in his paper, would wave an arm vaguely in their direction to show he was happy with the arrangement and Alison, grateful to these surrogate grandparents as she called them, saw a significant reduction in her day to day expenses.

To Reg's delight, Alison ran a coat of magnolia over the walls and paintwork so everywhere looked clean and inviting. Then, she bought contrasting throws and cushions in purple and burgundy to cover the three-piece suite and enjoyed personalising her surroundings with ornaments and photos. The Docklands flat became a distant memory and, when she did think back, she realised she'd never made any impression on it, which was further proof of how Richard had dominated her.

At work, Alison asked her colleagues to make excuses if Richard turned up and was glad she'd taken the precaution when she heard he'd been in a couple of times. Having made the break, she could see no point in meeting up again.

She also got in touch with her old flat mates who were huffy to start with, pointing out how quickly she'd dropped them when she'd met Richard; but, Alison worked hard to build bridges so before long 'The Bed-Sit Four' was back in business and it was fun getting dressed up to party in the local night-clubs.

'Richard and I hardly ever went out once we got engaged,' she'd shouted above the music one evening; and then made her friends laugh by adding: 'When we did it was always to a posh restaurant where the entertainment was listening to Richard spouting on about some spectacular deal he'd pulled off that day.'

Every three or four weeks she met Martin at a hotel they'd found in Surrey which, although closer in distance to Alison, took her as long to get to because of the traffic. She enjoyed these weekends until Martin started pushing for an answer about how much longer it would be before she returned to Southcliffe.

'I have to wait for the right position to come up and, when it does, I'll be back,' she'd say, fighting to hide her irritation; because, what with Winnie's ministrations and the discovery that membership of a commuter club would reduce travel costs, her initial financial concerns had been unfounded. And, when a further promotion led to a pay rise, she was in even less of a hurry to make changes.

But, she didn't mention any of this to Martin and the year came to an end without any sign of Alison leaving London.

CHAPTER 22

It didn't take long for Richard's life to settle into a pattern. His car had come back good as new and fortunately he'd got away with the alarm being switched off (had the assessor felt sorry for him and turned a blind eye?) However, the excess was still astronomical and payment seriously depleted his bank account.

Richard missed Alison and called in at the bank a couple of times to speak to her. But she was always 'busy with a client' so, after the third attempt, he gave up.

Being rejected brought back all the old insecurities.

Richard had been a prime target for bullies when growing up – the unfashionable glasses, geeky haircut and pompous attitude not helping.

At sixteen, he'd joined a swimming club in an attempt to lose the pounds gained as a studious teenager and, for a few weeks, practised obsessively in order to take part in a sponsored swimathon. He achieved his goal to swim a mile, but when his weight stayed the same, quit the club in disgust.

Although schooldays had been bleak, he

flourished once he got to university and, away from his mother's cooking, soon lost the flab. After exchanging glasses for contact lenses, he learned to cover shyness with assertiveness and left three years later with a first class degree. However, beneath the new found air of confidence, his self-esteem remained fragile.

When they first met, Alison had been a little in awe of him; but, she had an inborn assurance that grew as their courtship developed. She told him she'd also been a swat at school, but the bullies had left her alone.

They never really tried she'd laughed, when he'd wondered why that was. I suppose they knew what they'd get if they did ... of course it probably helped that Dad was one of the teachers.

When he'd asked how she'd have handled it if they had ganged up on her, she'd done that thing of lunging and pretending to bite his neck and they'd ended up in a tangle on the floor, the wrestling soon giving way to kissing.

Although he'd managed to conceal his lack of confidence in London, the cracks started to show as soon as he arrived in Southcliffe and the day he nearly crashed onto the beach was the first time he'd felt so inept for ages.

He shuddered each time he recalled Alison's exasperation. It had made him feel like a schoolboy again so, in an effort to wipe out the memory, he resolved to put all thoughts of his ex-fiancée out of his mind.

Soon after the New Year, Richard helped another girl move her belongings into his apartment. She was a little younger than Alison and also worked in a bank ... but as a cashier behind the counter.

The first time she saw the flat, her mouth fell open and Richard smiled as he draped an arm over her shoulders to show her round. His demons were back in their box and this time he was determined to keep it that way.

CHAPTER 23

Christmas had been a disappointment.

When Alison went back to see her parents for the holidays, neither she nor Martin had told anyone they were dating as there'd been an unspoken agreement between them to keep quiet about their relationship.

Martin's reason was simple. He didn't want to face anxious looks and questions from his mother ... especially as she was already suspicious. When he told her about the latest 'update weekend' arranged by the garage, she'd raised her eyebrows and said, 'What another one? That's one every month. Why so many courses? Surely, things don't change that quickly in the motor mechanic world?'

Alison didn't really know why she hadn't said anything to Fay and David. She was aware they'd been suspicious of Martin from the outset ... and all those allegations from Richard hadn't helped ... so she decided to say nothing about the regular meet ups in Surrey.

Consequently, Alison and Martin met briefly on Christmas morning, alongside Yuletide swimmers in fancy dress waiting for the annual dash into the sea, and left it at that.

***

As winter gave way to spring, Martin became more and more obsessed about getting Alison back to Southcliffe.

He knew she was enjoying London and, when she invited him to spend a weekend in the flat, he could see how fond she'd grown of Reg and Winnie. She introduced him as 'a friend from home' and the elderly couple had been warm and welcoming; but, on seeing how comfortable Alison was in their company, jealousy started to gnaw. Why would Alison want to rush back while she had those two to fuss round her?

She'd also told him about 'The Bedsit Four.' Honestly Martin, you wouldn't believe some of the things we get up to, she'd giggled one evening just as Martin was about leave. When we're together we behave like school kids. We nearly got thrown out of one club … but on second thoughts, I won't tell you about that. I don't think you'd approve.

Martin had tried to laugh with her, but inside he'd been fuming and his anger mounted when Alison started complaining about the drop in income she would suffer if she changed jobs. That was when he knew she was having second thoughts about returning home.

***

With Easter approaching, Alison was looking forward to visiting her parents. She'd felt bad about missing Mothers Day, but it had been the weekend she was due to meet Martin and he hadn't wanted to change it.

'I got tickets for that show you said you wanted to see,' he'd explained. 'They're for the Saturday and I thought we could spend the weekend at your flat ... sorry ... I hadn't noticed the date when I booked,' he'd added. 'But it's too late to change them now.'

Alison had phoned Fay to explain why she couldn't come down that weekend after all and sensed disappointment behind the bright assurances about how she mustn't feel guilty and how they would be looking forward to hearing all about the show when she did come four weeks later.

As it happened, the musical was every bit as good as the reviews and, during the interval, they were enjoying a drink in the bar when Alison felt her phone vibrate as a text came through. She nearly didn't check ... it was unlikely to be important ... but curiosity got the better of her and she frowned when she saw it was from Reg, saying nothing more than 'please ring.'

Reg hated the phone; he also knew she was at the theatre so something must be very wrong. Quickly, she pressed call, straining to hear the ringing tone above noisy chatter in the crowded bar.

'Hello ... is that Alison?' the worried voice sounded older over the phone.

'Hi Reg, is everything okay?'

'Oh, Alison, I'm so glad you got my message ... we've had a fire.'

'What?' Alison beckoned Martin over and switched to loudspeaker.

'The alarm went off about eight while we were watching television...'

There was a muffled voice that seemed to come from a distance.

'Reg? ... I can't hear you.'

'Sorry love; that was Winnie, wanting me to tell you she's fine ... anyway, when I went to look, the hall was full of smoke. It was coming from the kitchen so I shut the door, grabbed my phone ... and Winnie of course ... and we went out of the house. Thank God, the fire brigade came quickly so it didn't have a chance to spread.'

'How awful,' Alison put a hand to her pounding heart and stared at Martin who's eyes flicked briefly to a clock on the wall. 'Are you sure you're both all right?'

'Yes, yes; we're not hurt, but I thought I'd better tell you before you get back so you know what to expect. The kitchen will be out of action for a while, but everywhere else is okay.'

'Should we come back? The second half is about to start.'

'No, there's no need. You enjoy the rest of the show. There's nothing you can do here. Winnie's a bit shaken so I'm going to keep an eye on her, what with her angina. But, we're all right so don't worry.'

'Well ... if you're sure. We'll be back in a couple of hours anyway, so we'll see you then.'

Alison switched off her phone as she and Martin went back to their seats but, when the lights went down, she touched Martin's arm and, murmuring apologies, started to edge out of the row.

Back at the house, Reg told his story again while Alison, catching Winnie's reflection in a mirror saw her pop a pill under her tongue when she thought no one was looking.

Later that night, Winnie's chest pains worsened so Reg took her to hospital where they kept her in for observation.

CHAPTER 24

The following Monday, Alison called in to see Winnie on her way home from work and stopped for a moment to admire a magnolia tree, which was in full flower outside the hospital main entrance.

The stunning show of pink and white tulips reminded her of Southcliffe where Fay's tree would probably be in similar bloom and she remembered how her mother reckoned that magnolia was one of the first signs of spring. She sighed. Alison was always nostalgic for the sea once the better weather arrived.

After calling in at the shop, she headed for the ward, whilst thinking back to Saturday and realising again what a good job it was she hadn't gone to see her parents that weekend, after all. And thank goodness she'd made Reg buy those smoke alarms. It was the harrowing local TV coverage of a house fire that did it; the images of a distraught father unable to save his family, making an unexpected impact on her.

When she'd asked Reg a few days later if he'd fitted them, he'd said he'd been meaning to … probably ought to get them up, what with you being a paying tenant, he'd added … but, when he still didn't do it, she got them off Winnie and put them up herself.

In the ward, she found Winnie sitting up in bed looking quite perky. Reg also looked more relaxed and Alison was relieved to see their welcoming smiles as she approached.

'Hello, love,' Reg stood up to give her a kiss, 'thanks for dropping by ... is that for Winnie? Look Win, Alison's brought you some fruit.'

'Oh, that is kind, dear,' Winnie beamed as Alison stooped to kiss her cheek. 'And thanks for coming to see me. It seems I've been lucky, but the doctor said I must avoid stress or next time it might be a different story.'

'I'm so pleased you're all right,' Alison dropped into the chair Reg had drawn up for her and watched as he resumed his seat on the opposite side of the bed, taking Winnie's hand in both of his and kissing it.

'Yes, the doctor said if everything stays stable, I can go home tomorrow.'

'Well, I'm glad.' Alison took Winnie's other hand and clasped it tightly.

They chatted for a while and then, when a nurse came in to do the obs, Reg jumped out of his seat and beckoned Alison to follow. 'We'll get out of your way,' he said as the man wrapped a blood pressure cuff round his wife's arm and added, 'back in a minute, Win,' before heading to the window.

Reg's brow creased as Alison joined him and

he took her arm, turning her until they both faced away from the bed. 'I think I should tell you about the insurance claim,' he began and Alison noticed his voice had gone wavery

'They told me to go ahead and get quotes for repairs to the kitchen...'

'Well ... that's good, isn't it?' Something about the way Reg had begun to polish his glasses on a giant handkerchief, set butterflies fluttering in Alison's stomach.

'Yes, yes, that part's fine ... but they wanted to know how the fire started so I had to tell them what the chief fireman said.'

'Which was?'

'Apparently a gas ring had been left on 'simmer' and there was a tea towel close by that must have caught light. There was also a newspaper next to the towel and they were both under the kitchen roll holder. Once they all went up ...' Reg made an exploding gesture with his hands before mopping his face with the handkerchief.

'The thing is, Win gets upset so we don't talk about it; but, I know she's always careful about turning the gas off ... and we never leave papers by the cooker.'

Reg replaced his glasses and stuffed the hankie into an inside pocket of his jacket. 'Now, she thinks she's got memory problems as well as a dodgy ticker. She keeps talking about her mum who used to put the gas on then forget about it when she was beginning to get dementia. You wouldn't believe the number of saucepans she burned through. Win had to buy her a new one almost every week before she was eventually diagnosed.'

'Oh, I'm sure it's nothing like that,' Alison put an arm round her landlord's shoulders when she saw his distress. 'It was probably just an oversight and not likely to happen again.'

'That's what I told her,' Reg's eyes were bright with unshed tears. 'But it's really scared her and she's adamant she won't use the cooker unless I'm there to make sure it's safe.'

'Poor Winnie,' Alison looked over to where the nurse was scribbling results on a clipboard. 'She's obviously had a fright ... and poor you, as well. But, I'm sure you'll both be okay ... once the kitchen is back to normal.'

'I hope so.' Reg took out another handkerchief that Alison recognised as one of the monogrammed set she'd bought him for Christmas. 'This has really knocked us for six,' he said after blowing his nose loudly. 'I tell you what, though. It's a good job you got those damned alarms up. Things would have been much worse if we hadn't caught it when we did.'

Later that evening, after giving his wife a hug, Reg suppressed a shudder as he set off home.

Something had struck him when Alison and Martin came back from the theatre and he couldn't get it out of his head. He'd said then about being glad Alison put the alarms up and Martin's expression had slipped for a brief moment to reveal a definite scowl of annoyance. It had given Reg a real jolt.

He'd nearly mentioned it to Alison during their conversation, but hadn't been able to find the words. Knowing her short temper, she wouldn't take kindly to the insinuation and he dared not risk upsetting Winnie again because it would put her recovery right back.

And besides, why would Martin wish harm on them? He hardly knew them.

***

While Alison was visiting Winnie, Martin was back at work, thinking about the weekend just gone.

How furious would Alison have been if she'd known the real reason for choosing that day for the theatre? But, he'd had to do something to get away.

He hated Mother's Day. It was the hypocrisy he couldn't stand. Sentiments on cards bore no relation to the way he felt about his mother and he was sure she wouldn't believe a word of them either. The truth was they were both more comfortable if they avoided each other on days like that.

Martin started the engine of a Mitsubishi Outlander and listened to it with an expert ear.

Alison was due to come down for Easter and the issues surrounding her Christmas visit were still not resolved. He'd hoped they'd be living together by now and he knew it was only a matter of time before another 'Richard' caught her eye.

Annoyingly, his plan to take out one of the factors keeping her in London had failed; but it might have succeeded had Alison not installed those smoke alarms.

It wasn't that he had any particular desire to hurt Reg or Winnie, but they were helping to keep Alison there and he'd reasoned that, if the flat were out of the equation, maybe she'd come home.

Now he'd have to think of another way to get her back where she belonged; in Southcliffe with him.

CHAPTER 25

Alison was in a strange mood after leaving the hospital. She'd been pleased to see Winnie looking so much better, but something about Reg had disturbed her. She was sure he'd been going to say something else earlier, but then the nurse called them back and the moment passed.

The visit had also made Alison think again about her future. It would be so easy to let things stay as they were but, when she'd observed the friendly professionalism with which the hospital staff carried out their duties, she realised something was missing in her life.

For some reason it had reminded her of her father's talent for teaching... and of how she possessed similar skills; a discovery made when she worked with the local cub scouts a few years ago. She also remembered how the experience, albeit short lived, had given her a sense of fulfilment, which she'd never been able to achieve during her meteoric rise in the world of banking.

As she put the key in the lock of what she now regarded as her second home, Alison's thoughts turned to Winnie who had provided a shoulder to cry on while she was still getting over the break up with Richard. When she'd told her landlady how badly he'd behaved ... describing the accident at sea and his subsequent flight back to the city ... Winnie had done that rare thing of letting her talk without offering advice or relaying stories of her own experiences. Then she'd asked about the friends she'd lost touch with, which had prompted Alison to look them up.

Having a good social life, together with the set-up with Reg and Winnie and seeing Martin for the occasional weekend, was great; but, as she climbed the stairs to her flat, she began to see how maybe it was no longer enough. Was it time to move on?

Deep in thought, Alison made coffee and helped herself to a piece of Winnie's banana cake while picturing how her father would react if he knew the changes she was thinking of making to her life. And how pleased Martin would be when he found out she was definitely coming back to Southcliffe.

Alison's resolve grew quickly so that by the time she'd finished her snack, she'd made the decision to turn her back on banking and dip a toe into the world of teaching; and what's more, she would tell everyone during the Easter break. Then she would look into finding somewhere local to live.

Of course Reg and Winnie would be devastated, but the germ of an idea was beginning to form that might just keep everyone happy.

***

'... so you see we've been meeting every few weeks since I broke up with Richard and it's really working out well for us.'

It was Easter Sunday and, deciding to get the difficult part over first, Alison finally told Fay and David about Martin, blurting out the last bit out while staring defiantly at her parents.

Fay's tightly folded arms suggested she might be fighting the urge to shake some sense into her daughter. 'But, why have you only just got round to telling us?' she demanded. 'Didn't it seem strange that you felt you had to keep it secret all this time?'

'I didn't say anything because I knew neither of you would approve ... and I also wanted to see if our relationship would work before making a commitment ... but, we've been seeing each other for nine months now so I think we can prove we have something going for us.'

'Spending the odd weekend together doesn't prove anything,' retorted Fay. 'You have to live with someone twenty four/seven to be sure ... you know that from your experience with Richard.'

'I know Mum, and that brings me to my next bit of news. I'm going to move back to Southcliffe so I can be closer to Martin ... and Dad, I've decided to go into teaching after all and I'll do my training down here.'

Alison turned away from the expression on her father's face. 'I thought that's what you wanted,' she whispered, tears starting in her eyes.

'Of course it's what I want,' said David. 'You know that; but are you sure it's what **you** want? Last time we spoke you said you weren't interested in a career change ... and it won't pay as well as the bank. Also, have you thought how you're going to manage while you're training? ... Of course, our offer for you to stay here still stands,' he added.

'Yes, I know Dad, and I'm very grateful, but I've been doing a lot of thinking lately and I have an idea that may suit us all.

'Remember I told you about Reg and Winnie ... and the fire ... and Winnie's heart scare? ... Well, the thing is, they've lived in the same house since they got married and their children live abroad so they have no relatives close by.'

Alison caught the look that passed between her parents and knew they were bracing themselves for one of her impulsive schemes.

'You see, they've turned out to be like an extra set of grandparents and I know they look on me in the same way...'

'Get to the point.' Fay's voice sharpened as she glanced at her watch.

'Well ... when I leave, they'll miss me ... and I'll definitely miss them ... but what if they were to move down here as well?'

Fay's eyebrows shot up. 'What?-'

'-You see, they own the house and would get a good price because it's an easy commute to London ... and, if they bought a similar property here, it would cost less and leave them with money in the bank. I could continue to rent from them, which would be great for all of us ... and...'

Alison fiddled with the fringe on a cushion, reluctant now to share the last part of her plan.

'And?'

'And, Martin could come and live with me so he can help with the rent while I'm not earning.'

A clock ticking on the mantelpiece sounded loud in the silence that followed.

'Hmm ... what do Reg and Winnie think?'

Annoyed that her mother had picked up straight away on a possible snag, Alison sighed. 'Well, I wanted to speak to you before I put the idea to them. I can't ask them to consider such a step without letting them see Southcliffe first so I wondered if they could come and stay here for a week. They'd be no trouble, and they both love the sea, so maybe they'll realise Southcliffe has more to offer than where they are at the moment.'

Fay and David exchanged a different kind of look and her mother's voice softened as she spoke for them both. 'Yes, of course they can come. Even if they decide not to move, it would be a holiday and I'd be only too happy to show them the local sights.'

'It would also give us a chance to thank them for looking after you,' added David, putting an arm round his daughter's shoulders.

Alison leaned against her father and kissed his cheek; she'd known that part would be okay and was steeling herself for the inevitable follow up question.

'And Martin?' Fay's tone had cooled again. 'How does he feel about it?'

'Well, I haven't said anything to him either.' Alison suppressed her exasperation as she saw their relief. 'I wanted to see what Reg and Winnie decide first. I've told Martin about the teaching and he's pleased about that. But, I think he's assuming I'll live here.'

At that moment, Alison's mobile rang and she left the room to answer it.

'Saved by the bell,' commented Fay, sinking into an armchair. 'That's all a bit unlikely, isn't it?'

'Certainly is,' said David. 'I can't imagine Reg and Winnie will want to move away from where they've lived all their married lives ... especially at their age.'

But David didn't know Reg and Winnie.

CHAPTER 26

Alison floated the idea to her landlords as soon as she got back after the Easter holiday. 'What do you think? She asked.

Reg polished his spectacles energetically. 'Well ... it would need thinking about.'

'Yes, I realise that,' said Alison. 'But, why not come down and stay with Mum and Dad for a holiday? You've nothing to lose and if you decide you don't want to move, that's fine. I promise I won't put pressure on you.'

'There's no harm in that, Reg,' pleaded Winnie.

'No, I suppose not.' Unable to find a good reason without offending Alison, Reg nodded and so it was arranged.

***

Reg and Winnie loved Southcliffe.

Fay took them to all the local attractions and, although it was still early in the season, the weather was warm so they were able to enjoy walks on the beach followed by lunch in various pub gardens, most of which overlooked the sea.

Winnie rated everything perfect and by the end of the week, Reg had come round to her way of thinking.

Fay took them to an estate agent before they went home and almost immediately they found a bungalow, complete with annexe, which they both fell in love with. The annexe was a detached smaller version of the bungalow and would be ideal for Alison to live in while she did her training.

They knew she would probably move into her own house eventually, but Reg and Winnie were sure they'd be able to rent the annexe out as a holiday flat when that time came; and it was separate from the main bungalow so there would be little or no inconvenience.

Once the decision was made, everything moved rapidly. Reg and Winnie's property was sold to the first viewer, who also paid the asking price, and Reg was flabbergasted at how the house had appreciated in value.

'I can't believe we've been sitting on all that money,' he said to Winnie as they signed the contracts. 'Who'd have thought it?'

***

By the middle of August Reg, Winnie and Alison had settled into their new homes.

Winnie had expected to feel sad when she closed the door of their marital home for the last time, but the kitchen fire had changed everything and all she saw was bricks and mortar. Her home was already packed up and she would re-create it in the new bungalow.

She felt a thrill of excitement. She'd never imagined they would ever move and now she was on the brink of a new life by the sea.

CHAPTER 27

'I know we had our doubts about Martin, but he seems to be making Alison happy.' Busy emptying the dishwasher, Fay didn't see the shadow pass over her husband's face. 'And he's certainly a different person when she's around. He even makes jokes.'

'One joke, as I recall,' said David. 'Something about how Reg and Winnie should be living in the Granny annexe instead of Alison ... and it wasn't that funny.'

Fay shut the cutlery drawer and started on the plates. 'Well, everyone laughed.'

'Probably because it's the one time Martin's ever said anything remotely amusing ... and it was only Winnie and Alison who laughed; Reg never cracked a smile; I'm not sure he's that struck on him.'

'No, you're right.' Fay frowned. 'He always seems a bit cool when Martin's around.' She shut the dishwasher door and wiped it over with a tea towel. 'Anyway, I'm off now to my yoga class. I'll see you later.'

David had given Fay an absent-minded kiss as she passed and was now thinking back to how he'd disappointed Alison with his reaction when she said she was going into teaching. But, it was only because his happiness had been spoiled by the discovery that her one time teenage sweetheart was definitely back in her life.

'Take my advice; don't let Alison get caught up with Martin again...' He still remembered Richard's words. And he hadn't forgotten the chill that ran through him on the drive home from London when he'd linked Martin to incidents, which could have had fatal consequences.

***

Martin may have smiled when he made his crack about the Granny annexe, but he wasn't laughing inside.

The last year had been hard and he'd lived only for the weekends spent with Alison. In between had been emptiness, broken by dark thoughts, with Richard at the centre of these imaginings. He knew Alison had lost touch with her former fiancé, but still he fantasised about finishing what he'd started last July. Leaving aside the fact he was nearly caught ... or maybe because of it ... the 'accident' at sea had given him a real buzz ... and so had trashing the car.

Now, Richard was out there with a hidden memory, which could return at any time. But, knowing he could still be challenged wasn't why he was obsessed. It was more about unfinished business between them.

And thinking of unfinished business, he was painfully aware that his failed attempt to get rid of the new interlopers in Alison's life had led to a situation where they were still a cosy threesome; the only difference being that Reg and Winnie were living here now, rather than London. A further irony was that Alison had said how the fire, and subsequent visit to see Winnie in hospital, had started her thinking about a career change.

The only good thing to come out of it was that he no longer had to wait four weeks between meetings.

***

Alison had managed to find part time work at a local restaurant, when she discovered the newly appointed manager was a friend she'd known since they were in nursery together, and her income would just about cover the cut down rent her landlords had set. But, she still hadn't asked Martin if he'd like to move in with her although she'd mentioned the possibility to Reg and Winnie to make sure they didn't mind.

Winnie had been fine. 'I don't see why not,' she'd said. 'You're a couple and it would make sense to share living costs.'

Reg, however, had scrubbed at his glasses and said something about reducing the rent further if it was too much for her while she was training. 'After all,' he'd added, 'it's because of you that we have a bit put by so we don't need the money so much now, do we Win?'

'No, of course not, dear.'

Winnie, bless her, would always back her husband, but she'd looked surprised at the suggestion and Alison had noticed how Reg seemed to be sharing the same reservations about Martin as her parents.

Wondering why that should be, she acted on a gut feeling and decided to leave things as they were for now. Besides, her father had also offered a temporary allowance to help her through training so she wasn't as dependent on Martin's input as she'd expected to be.

Also, the annexe wasn't really big enough for both of them as, once she'd unpacked her things from London and collected some of the stuff her parents had been storing, there was little room for anything else.

Then there'd be the studying and she wouldn't be able to concentrate with someone else there ... especially if it was Martin.

A quiver ran through her when she thought back to their weekends in Surrey. Maybe if they avoided the humdrum side of living together it would help keep those feelings alive.

CHAPTER 28

When Alison received confirmation of a place in college some ten miles away, she had a rare moment of uncertainty. Was this what she really wanted? Would she miss the hustle and bustle of working in London? She brushed away the doubt and tried to concentrate on how much she enjoyed being by the sea and on how fortunate she was that Reg and Winnie had moved down with her.

Also, she reasoned, if it really didn't work out, she could go back and pick up her career in banking again ... as long as she didn't leave it too long.

***

There'd been a bit of time to wait before Alison started her training so Martin booked leave from the garage and they spent the days swimming, walking and making love in the little annexe. The weather stayed warm and he was able to put shadowy thoughts on hold, unaware that his mother had been watching and hoping her son's rare period of happiness would last.

When Alison's course began, Martin resented having to go back to seeing her less often and that was when he seriously thought about asking her to marry him; but fear of rejection prevented him from popping the question. He knew, even if she accepted, David and Fay would try to dissuade her and he was also aware that Reg had developed a bit of an attitude too. It had started around the time they'd gone to the theatre in the spring and Martin wondered if he suspected anything; but why would he since he and Alison had been miles away when the fire broke out.

***

Fay enjoyed introducing her new friend to the delights of the small seaside town and Winnie embraced all of it, from the WI activities ... 'I never realised they did such interesting stuff ...' to a weekly aquarobics class.

'We do it all to something called zumba music,' she'd explained to Alison, who'd been a bit concerned.

Don't go overdoing it,' she'd warned. 'Remember you're not used to it.'

'Don't worry,' Fay had reassured her daughter. 'I'm keeping a close eye on her and we got the okay from the GP.'

Within a short while Winnie's fitness levels had improved and frequent walks along the sea front with Reg meant she was less reliant on medication now.

'So much more pleasant than trudging round streets,' she told Fay one day when they'd gone for a morning coffee together. 'I just wish our boys were here too. I'm sure the granddaughters would love the beach, even though we haven't got the weather they've got.'

'Yes, Alison said your children live abroad.' Fay suppressed a shudder as she tried not to think about how devastated she'd be if Alison decided to emigrate. 'Whereabouts are they?'

Well, the eldest went to Australia for his gap year and has been in Melbourne ever since ... he married an Australian and they have two teenage daughters.'

'How sad you don't see them. have you been out there?'

'We went once ... just after Ellie was born; such a sweet little thing.' Winnie dabbed away a tear. 'We'd have gone again, but the journey was too much so I don't know when we'll see them now.'

'And your other son?'

'Also married and on secondment in Canada. We're hoping they may come back at some point and maybe start a family? At least we have Skype and Facetime, and of course having Alison in our lives has been a great bonus. We're both so glad she chose to rent from us when she broke up with her fiance.

***

Reg was also pleased with his new surroundings, especially as he now had a sea view to enjoy from the summerhouse.

It's a bit different from all that concrete we used to look out on,' he said, accepting the beer David handed him in the local pub one evening. 'And I never get tired of watching the sea.'

It was kind of David to to take him out for the occasional half pint. Reg wasn't a big drinker, but David was good company and he liked being introduced to the regulars, many of whom were also retired.

Tonight it was just the two of them and David was telling him about Alison's new life as a trainee teacher.

'I can't tell you how glad I am she decided to do it,' David handed Reg a packet of pork scratchings and opened a bag of smokey bacon crisps for himself. 'The bank was okay, but Alison was always going to grow out of it. She's a 'giving something back' girl at heart and banking was never going to satisfy her in the long term.

'You're right about her being a 'giving something back' girl, said Reg. 'She certainly worked miracles in the flat when she moved in and we were always saying how lucky we were to have her as a tenant ...You won't tell Win about these, will you?' He took a mouthful of the savoury treat and waved the bag at David.

'Not if you promise to keep quiet about these,' replied David, shaking his crisp packet. 'They're not exactly Fay's idea of healthy food.'

They munched in companionable silence for a minute or two, then David asked: 'What do you think of Martin?'

Reg hesitated before taking a blue hankie out of his pocket to clean his glasses. He was trying to picture times when David and Martin were together, but could only remember the day they all helped Alison move into the annexe. Martin had made a joke - unusual for him - but only the women had laughed.

'I don't know him that well,' he parried cautiously. 'Why, what do you think of him?'

'Hmm, that's a good question; and, if I'm honest, I have concerns. He has traits that worry me.'

'Oh?' Reg looked up warily. 'What sort of traits?'

'I won't go into details, but let's just say bad things have a habit of happening when Martin's around.'

Reg nearly choked on his beer.

'Are you all right?' David got up to pat him on the back. 'Should I get you some water?'

'No, I'm fine,' gasped Reg. 'It's just what you said ...'

'Did I strike a chord?' ... Reg, if something's happened that involves Martin, it's really important you tell me.'

'Well, I don't know what to think ...' Reg had gone back to polishing his spectacles. 'I thought it was my imagination; now, I'm not so sure ... but, I don't see how Martin could have...'

'Could have what?'

Reg described the night of the fire.

'... when Alison and Martin got back from the theatre, I mentioned how it was a good job the alarms had been set up and there was a really strange look on his face. It only lasted second - you know how po-faced he is - but it gave me the jitters. No-one else saw it ... and I certainly wasn't going to tell Win, what with her palpitations ... but for a momentI got the feeling he might have set the fire himself.' Reg mopped his face with the handkerchief. 'There, now I've said it ... and you think I'm crazy.'

'Think carefully, Reg. Is there any way Martin could have done that?'

Reg sipped at what was left of his beer. 'You're not saying you believe me are you?' When David didn't reply, he added, 'Well, like I say, I don't see how he could have.'

'Think back, urged David, 'and take me through everything that happened.'

'Reg went over it again and this time added what the fireman had said. 'But, it didn't make sense. Winnie's so careful ... and if it was her memory, wouldn't other odd things be happening?'

David frowned and nodded. 'Reg, could Martin possibly have come back after they left for the theatre? What were you and Winnie doing that evening?'

'Watching TV,' said Reg, 'We put a quiz show on ... and I remember that night because Winnie said, much as she loved Alison, she was glad they'd gone so she could watch it properly. We have the volume quite loud these days and don't always hear above it - especially if the door's shut - so I suppose he could have come back.

***

A few days later, Alison popped in to see her parents, but only David was home.

'So, how's it going?' he said, after giving his daughter a kiss, 'Your mother's down at the gym so we can talk shop without being tedious.'

Alison needed no second bidding and before long they were involved in a heated discussion about discipline in schools and how things had changed over the last half century.

'Whoa!' said David eventually, holding his hands up to stop the flow. 'I can see things have moved on a lot since my training days. Let's agree to disagree and change the subject.'

Alison stopped mid sentence. 'Oh ... all right then. But, this is the way things are going and you'll have to embrace it sometime-'

'-Yes, I know,' smiled David, 'but, maybe not today?'

Alison laughed. 'You'll be a dinosaur soon; you know that don't you?'

David clawed his hands, making roaring noises until she ran away in mock fear and he was pleased he could still make his daughter laugh.

'I'm so glad you're enjoying the course,' he said after chasing her round the room twice before collapsing out of breath onto the sofa. 'But, don't you miss anything about being in London ... theatre trips for instance?'

'No, not really,' Alison threw herself down beside him and linked arms. 'We didn't go as often as I'd have liked because Richard wasn't that keen...'

Alison's brow creased. 'Actually, the last time I went was with Martin. I'd been planning to to come home that weekend, but he booked tickets for 'Chicago' without realising it was Mother's Day.' She rested her head on David's shoulder. 'It was funny really ... it's always me who arranges outings ... but that time he organised it all by himself.'

She smiled fondly at the memory. 'Mind you, it nearly didn't happen. Martin's usually so meticulous, but we were halfway to the station before he realised he'd forgotten to pick up the tickets. You stay here and I won't be a minute, he said ... but he was gone ages and when he got back he seemed really jumpy. He hates being caught out ... Dad? you've gone all tense. Are you all right?'

'Yes, love, 'course I am ... now, are you going to stay until your mother gets back? She shouldn't be long. Tell me more about your course while we're waiting.'

David half listened to another lecture, but his thoughts were elsewhere. There were too many coincidences to ignore now. But, what should he do? ... If only Richard could remember what had happened after his fateful boat trip.

'But, he might now.' David hadn't realised he was speaking out loud.

'Pardon?' Alison stopped in the middle of telling him about gender identity and LGBT+ rights.

'Oh, nothing ... I was just thinking Reg might have changed his mind about going to the pub tonight.'

'Sorry if I'm boring you.'

'No, of course you're not, said David, 'but don't forget I've been dealing this a lot longer than you have.'

'I hardly think so,' Alison's eyes widened. 'These issues are relatively recent and very complex. There are no easy solutions.'

The sound of a key in the door announced Fay's return and David, who had no idea what his daughter had been talking about, stood up and pulled Alison to her feet.

'We must discuss it at length sometime,' he said, putting an arm round her. 'I could do with fresh viewpoints to counter my cynicism ... but not now. Let's see if we can get your mother to rustle up some lunch.

'Okay,' laughed Alison. 'I can see I've got some converting to do ... but i agree; lunch first.'

She followed her father out of the room to join Fay in the kitchen.

CHAPTER 29

Towards the end of October, Alison managed to take a few days off college by juggling her study periods and Martin booked leave enabling them to spend time together. But the weather was cold and rainy so by Wednesday, both were fed up with being indoors.

'Have you done any paddle boarding?' Martin had been pacing the room and looking out of the window. 'I can't stand the thought of doing nothing all day.'

'I don't call what we've just done 'doing nothing.'' Alison's eyes misted over at the memory. 'But, no, paddle boarding is not something I've ever tried. Is it hard?'

'Not really ... well, perhaps a bit tricky at first. It's a knack, but once you get the hang of it, it's fine. D'you fancy having a go? It's not windy so conditions are okay for a beginner.'

'Why not?' Alison glanced out at the low clouds. 'If nothing else it will feel great to come back into a warm room again, later.' She dug out her wet suit and they collected Martin's gear on the way to the beach.

Alison soon mastered the technique and when they finally came in from the sea, she couldn't believe how the time had flown. 'That was fun,' she said, 'but I thought you said it was difficult.'

Martin smiled one of his rare smiles. 'Obviously not for you; glad you enjoyed it.'

They spent the rest of the week out on the waves and, when a breeze sprang up Martin introduced her to kite surfing. The sport was very popular and Alison soon discovered how the rush of wind in her hair while soaring across the bay on the strings of a sail, was far more exciting than the snail pace of a paddleboard.

She also noticed how Martin was at his best by the sea. He never seemed to feel the cold and the joy on his face as he skimmed the waves was a complete contrast to his usual manner.

Like Richard - but for other reasons - Alison could see how different Martin was from most men his age. However, it concerned her that he had no friends because it led to their relationship being intense and this was reinforced by a conversation they had soon after she'd started her course.

'But, it makes more sense,' she'd argued. 'Surely you can see that if Ben and I share the petrol it halves the cost ... and we only have to find one parking space. They're like gold dust at the college so I don't see what the problem is.'

'Well, I could take you if you don't want to drive.' With hands thrust deep in his pockets, Martin had hunched his shoulders sullenly.

'What about getting back?'

'I could pick you up as well.'

'And, exactly how would that would that fit in with your work?' Alison raised her shoulders in an exasperated shrug. 'Honestly, Martin, you can't ferry me around. It's not practical … nor does it make sense financially.'

In the end, Alison insisted on the arrangement and travelled to and from college most days with her student friend. But, she knew Martin wasn't happy about it and she didn't like the way he scowled each time Ben's name was mentioned.

***

Martin had been furious when Alison insisted on travelling with another student. He knew his suggestion to drive her was unrealistic, but the thought of her being in a car with a younger man who shared her interests, was too much.

It was starting to happen; just like he knew it would; Alison was living in a different world and it was only a matter of time before someone stole her again.

The only way to stop it was to get a ring on her finger and he decided to risk a proposal on her birthday, just before Christmas. He knew she wouldn't agree to marry until she'd finished her course, but an engagement ring would have to do for now.

Then, he could suggest they find somewhere

to live together; Alison had been right about the annexe being too small. Besides, he needed to get her away from Reg and Winnie. There was something about Reg's manner that was starting to trouble him and the sooner Alison was free from their influence the better.

CHAPTER 30

David and Fay went to Tenerife for the October half-term break. Relaxing with a glass of wine by the hotel pool one afternoon while Fay swam, David went over all the incidents that might have involved Martin. Had he been responsible for the kitchen fire? Was a more sinister version of the accident at sea, locked up in Richard's memory? Did Martin attack his car? And Tim's accident ... did he fall into the road or was he pushed?

Later that term, David had an unexpected opportunity to make further enquiries into the last episode when Year seven had a Christmas disco on the first Friday in December. He usually managed to avoid these events, but this year one of the organisers went down with appendicitis and David had to step in to prevent the whole thing from being cancelled.

At the end of the evening, he was in charge of making sure all the children were reunited with their parents and soon the crowds thinned until only a handful were left. David didn't know any of them and asked one for her name.

'Tamsin Burgess,' said the girl.

The name rang a bell and that was when it all

came back. How could he have forgotten the sequel to what had been such a big topic of conversation in the staff room?

Tim Burgess had left hospital after recovering from his injuries, to discover that his girlfriend Grace was pregnant. They were only fifteen when the baby was born, but they'd made a go of it ... and the child would be around eleven or twelve now.

'Is your dad called Tim?' Asked David.

'Yes,' said Tamsin. 'He's coming to pick me up and said he might be a bit late as he's been working.'

As she spoke, a van drew up with a squeal of tyres and Tim jumped out. 'Sorry I'm late,' he gasped, sprinting over. 'I got held up.'

'That's okay,' said David. 'I know it's difficult when work is involved.'

'Well, Gracie would've come, but she's looking after the little ones. We have four children now,' he added proudly.

'My goodness; that was quick work. Congratulations.'

'Thanks ... I used to go to this school. You taught me a few times.'

'Yes, I remember.' David paused. All the children in his charge had been collected and there would never be another opportunity. 'As I recall, you were involved in a road accident when you were in Year nine or ten. I hope you made a full recovery?'

'Yes, I did, thanks, but it was bad at the time.'

'Do you remember much about it? ... I mean, how did you fall under the car that day?'

'Tammy, go and wait in the van,' said Tim. 'I'll be there in a moment.' He threw her the keys and they watched as she clambered into the passenger seat.

'Tams doesn't know about it,' he explained. 'Why are you asking, Mr. Albright? It was all such a long time ago.'

'I know,' said David, 'and I do have a reason. You may not remember of course, but if you think you were deliberately pushed, I might be able to stop similar incidents happening in the future ... if you see what I mean.'

'No, I don't see what you mean ... but I do think I was pushed.'

David let his breath out slowly. 'Okay ... and do you have any idea who may have done it?'

'Not really,' Tim frowned. 'As I remember, there were five or six kids close by so it could have been any of them ... or maybe someone further away pushed one on to me.'

'Hmm,' David played for time, not wanting to put words into his mouth. 'Do you remember which kids were there?'

'It's difficult,' Tim was glancing at his watch under the security light. 'There was quite a crowd, but I know Martin Landon was there. He and I used to hang out before I met Grace so I felt a bit bad that I'd dropped him ... but it really was love at first sight with me and Gracie...'

Tim flushed before looking away and David smiled.

'I do understand, Tim. It was the same with me and my wife.'

'Oh. Well then, you know what it's like.' Tim shrugged. 'I guess I didn't want to do all that stuff with Martin anymore. He was a bit miffed, but I hadn't seen him for a while ... and he was a loner so it was unusual for him to be in a big crowd.'

There was a sharp toot on the horn of Tim's van.

'Tamsin's getting impatient,' said Tom. 'I'd better go. It was nice to meet you again, Mr. Albright.'

'And you Tim ... and please, call me David.'

'Okay.' Tim grinned. "Bye, David.'

"Bye, Tim.' David waved them off and walked back to the car. Turning the ignition key, he drove out of the school grounds, deep in thought.

CHAPTER 31

Next morning, after Fay had gone shopping, David hunted for Richard's telephone number. Fay was constantly editing the home phone contact list and the only other place she might have put it was in her old address book, which David had given her when they first met. Nothing was ever erased from that. He was about to give up the search when it fell out of a pile of magazines and, quickly finding Richard's name, he scribbled down both the London landline and mobile number on the back of an envelope.

He checked his watch. Fay would want to know why he was getting in touch after all this time but, not wishing to share his concerns and knowing she wouldn't be back for at least an hour, David dialled the London number.

'Richard Clancy.' The voice sounded deeper on the phone.

'Hello Richard, this is David Albright,' he paused, 'Alison's father.'

'Hello David,' Richard chuckled down the line. 'Yes, I know who you are. What can I do for you? Is Alison all right?'

'Yes, she's fine.' David made a quick decision.

Fay would be busy most of the day and it would be awkward discussing things over the phone. 'Richard, I know this is going to sound strange, but I wondered if I could come up and see you. There's something I want to talk to you about.'

'It's about Martin, isn't it? Has something else happened?'

'Well, I'd rather talk face-to-face,' David hesitated. 'Look, I know its short notice, but I've got a free day and could be with you by mid afternoon. It wouldn't take long ... that is, if you could spare me an hour?'

'I could spare you more than an hour,' Richard sounded cheerful. 'In fact, why don't you stay the night? You don't really want to do that drive twice in one day and my girlfriend is visiting her parents this weekend ... I'm on my own and could use the company ... What d'you say?'

'Well...' David hesitated.

'There's a great restaurant nearby so you won't have to put up with my cooking. It'll be my treat.'

'You've talked me into it,' said David. 'Thanks, I'll see you later then.'

'Great, see you later.'

David put the phone down. Fay would be livid when she found out he'd stayed in that fabulous flat without her, but he couldn't involve her just yet. He packed a change of clothes, wrote a note promising to ring her later and left before she got back from her shopping trip.

It was four o'clock when David finally pulled into a visitor's parking space outside Richard's flat. The traffic had been awful and David realised, too late, that he'd hit the weekend pre-Christmas crowds.

Richard greeted him with a drink and David noticed the flat was looking more lived in than last time he'd been there. The current girlfriend had obviously made her mark in a way that Alison hadn't and Richard was also more relaxed than he'd been at Southcliffe.

David had wondered what they'd find to talk about, but he needn't have worried. Richard rattled on non-stop and David couldn't help but notice the difference between him and Martin. Strange that Alison should go from one extreme to the other, he thought.

Later, they walked down to a restaurant that overlooked the river and Richard treated David to a superb meal. Between courses, David heard all about the world of stock-broking and found it fascinating. His career as a teacher seemed boring by comparison, but he knew he wouldn't want it any other way. He'd have burnt out in a matter of weeks trying to live that sort of life.

After the meal, they moved to comfy seats by the window, beyond which the river flowed, and Richard ordered coffee. 'Right,' he said, settling back in his chair. 'I've done all the talking. It's your turn now. You must have had a good reason for driving all that way ... especially this time of year.'

David had been so wrapped up in Richard's conversation - and the best steak and French-fries he'd had in ages - that it took a moment to put his thoughts in order.

'I'm guessing it's to do with Martin?' said Richard, helpfully.

'Well, yes it is,' said David. 'The thing is, I was wondering if you ever recovered the memory of what caused your plunge into the sea last summer. Last time we spoke, you said you were sure Martin was to blame.'

'Yes, I did, didn't I?' said Richard. 'And I stand by that. The trouble is, I still can't remember. It's there under the surface because sometimes I get a glimmer; then it goes again. It's very frustrating.' He frowned. 'But why are you asking after all this time?'

Apart from Reg, David hadn't talked to anyone about his suspicions, but it occurred to him that someone ought to know ... and Richard was probably a good person to confide in. Alison had said he'd toyed with the idea of joining the police and it would be interesting to see what he made of it.

Richard listened without interrupting as David went through his list of 'co incidences' regarding Martin, then he gave a low whistle.

'Putting it all together makes it creepy, doesn't it?'

'Mmm,' said David. 'That's what I thought.'

They were silent while Richard refilled their cups. 'I had an interesting conversation with the trailer driver just after you and Alison left in the summer,' he commented while chasing an irregular shaped sugar lump round the bowl with impossibly small tongs. 'You remember? They came to pick up the Porsche?'

'Ah, yes,' David reached for his coffee. 'How is the car?'

'Fine now,' Richard threw down the tongs and used his fingers, 'but it cost a fortune.

'I think the trailer guy must have swallowed a psychology textbook because he was all set to lecture me on the extent of damage. He reckoned a lot of anger had gone into the attack and that I was lucky the intruder found the car and not me.' Richard took a sip of coffee and rolled it round his mouth before swallowing. 'I have to say I felt spooked; particularly so soon after my near fatal accident the week before.'

'I'm not surprised.'

'The thing is...' Richard hesitated. 'I've got a friend who's into criminology ... I just wanted to follow up what the trailer guy said,' he added when David's eyebrows lifted in surprise.

'Oh yes,' said David. 'And what did your friend say?'

'Well ... he talked about theories on why

some children turn out to be violent. You saying about the incident with Tim brought it to mind.'

David listened with interest. He'd been thinking more about whether Martin was responsible rather than why he'd done it. 'What sort of theories?' he asked.

'He believes that some kids grow up unable to recognise that other people have needs as well as themselves.'

David chuckled. 'In my experience, most children are self-centred.'

'Yes, that's true. But, usually they start to understand they're not the centre of the universe by the time they reach their teens.'

'I can think of a few people in my school who haven't reached that stage yet,' laughed David, 'and that's in the teaching staff, never mind the pupils. But I take your point. Martin was around fourteen at the time of Tim's accident and your friend would say he should have been able to control his anger, without pushing his one-time pal under a car.'

'Mmm ... I think what he actually said was...' Here, Richard stared into the middle distance as he tried to dredge up the exact words. '"Self-centredness persists, if moral development is atrophied." At least, it was something like that.

'I think he meant that some kids who have it all their own way at home, find it hard when it doesn't happen in the outside world. They get frustrated, then angry and lash out at anyone who upsets them.'

'If it's in the way, get rid of it?' hazarded David.

'Yes, I suppose so.' Richard took another mouthful of coffee. 'Of course there are lots of recognised syndromes now that maybe he didn't factor in.'

'You have been mugging up, haven't you? But, I'm not sure Martin fits into any of those categories; although Alison would probably be a better person to ask as her training is more up to date and she's always stressing how we as teachers should be putting coping strategies in place for children who have difficulty fitting in.'

'Has she ever considered how Martin might have 'difficulty fitting in?''

David's eyes widened. 'I don't think she thinks of him in those terms.'

'A bit surprising, isn't it; especially as she's covering all that stuff on her course?' Richard was starting to sound petulant.

'Well, perhaps Martin behaves differently with her.'

Richard shrugged. 'If you say so; its way out of my field. What sort of upbringing did he have?'

'No idea,' said David. 'His mother seems like a nice woman. Martin was a late baby - I think Fay said they'd pretty much given up hope when she fell pregnant - and Ruth is probably in her sixties now.'

'What about the father? What's he like?'

'I've never met him ... and Martin never talks about him ... nor does he say much about his mum, come to think of it. What else did your friend say?'

'Only how kids tend to copy aggressiveness and the first act of hostility is the hardest.

'Of course, he could be a psychopath. They're cunning and lacking in empathy ... so he definitely shows some of the characteristics.'

David's stomach lurched. 'Hang on, Richard; I'm not sure we're in that territory.'

'Tell that to people who've lived next door to a murderer without having a clue about who they really were until it was too late.'

As David swallowed the last of his coffee, he could feel his heart racing. Richard had given him plenty to think about and he resolved to do some research of his own when he got back to Southcliffe.

Back at the flat, David got to use the old fashioned bath with its fantastic view.

Taking his mobile out of his pocket, he realised he'd never rung Fay; neither had he switched the phone back on after his drive to London. Damn! Fay would be frantic. It was too late to call now so he sent a text telling her not to worry and saying he would be in touch in the morning, but the phone rang just as he was stepping into the bath and he was glad he'd kept it with him.

'Hello, Fay.'

'Where are you? I've been trying to get hold of you all day. Why did you go off without saying where you were going?'

'Sorry about that,' David lowered himself into the warm water. 'Something urgent came up and I had to deal with it.'

'What was so 'urgent' that you couldn't wait for me to get home ... and where are you now?' Fay's voice was shrill with worry.

'I'm okay. I'm in London and will be back tomorrow.'

There was a pause.

'Why are you in London? ... And where in London, are you?'

'I'm actually taking a bath in Richard's flat at the moment.' David chuckled as he pictured his wife's face.

After another silence, Fay's voice had come down a notch. 'Just what are you doing in Richard's bathroom?'

'I've told you ... taking a bath. I know it sounds ridiculous, but I really can't say any more over the phone. You'll just have to trust me on this and I promise I'll tell you everything when I get back.

'Incidentally, I'm on my own and the door is securely locked. Richard's girlfriend is away and he asked me to stay so I didn't have to drive here and back in one day.'

David heard a sniff at the other end of the phone and wasn't sure if she was crying, or just didn't believe a word. 'Look Fay, how often do I do things like this?'

'It's not like you,' admitted Fay, eventually.

'Right then; just be patient and all will be revealed tomorrow.'

'Tomorrow it is then and it had better be good ... Anyway, what's it like in Richard's bath?'

'Well, there's a view of the city, which in itself must cost a fortune. I can see the light blinking on top of Canary Wharf. But, I wouldn't change it for our sea view ... by the way; do you know anything about Martin's dad?'

'Matthew?' Fay sounded surprised. 'Only that he's not been seen for years. I think he disappeared when Martin was about eleven. The story was he went to visit relatives, but never returned ... Why do you ask?'

'Oh, I'll tell you when I see you,' said David. 'Right now, I'm going to find out what Richard's spare bed is like. See you tomorrow. Bye, love.'

''Bye,' said Fay. 'Give my regards to Richard and mind how you drive back.'

Well, that went better than I expected, thought David as he sank further into the warm water. But he knew Fay would want to know every detail once he got back to Southcliffe.

CHAPTER 32

David slept well and it was nearly nine o'clock before he opened his eyes, sniffing appreciatively at the smell of bacon frying.

After shrugging into a dressing gown that he found hanging on the bedroom door, he went to the kitchen where Richard was busy at the aga.

'Good morning David, hope you slept well. I do a mean breakfast ... full English, with all the trimmings?'

'Rather,' said David, and realised how pleasant it was to do something spontaneous for a change. He loved his life, but couldn't deny he was in a rut. 'I spoke to Fay last night and asked about Martin's dad,' he added, taking a seat at the table. 'She thinks he took off when Martin was a kid. I wonder if that's significant.'

'Could be,' said Richard. 'It means he had no role model when he was in his teens ... unless someone else stepped in?'

'I don't think so. As far as I know Ruth's never been connected with another man.'

After they'd eaten, David got dressed and packed his things, ready for the journey home.

'Look, you're going to be in the car most of the day and it's a lovely morning,' said Richard.

D'you fancy a walk through the park before you head off? There's a café on the riverbank where we could get coffee.'

'Why not?' said David. Richard obviously didn't want to be on his own and he was in no particular hurry. 'As long as I'm on the road by lunchtime; I'll put my stuff in the car as we go past then I can leave as soon as we get back.'

The sky was that brilliant blue that often goes with cold sunny days and frost on the grass glistened like diamonds as David and Richard walked to the café. After ordering coffee, they sat by a window overlooking the water's edge and watched as people went by enjoying the fine weather.

A group of lads were jostling and laughing as they meandered along. Then one boy picked up a handful of stones and started skimming them across the water. Soon the others joined in and an impromptu game began to see who could get the most bounces out of their stones.

David turned to say how he used to enjoy doing that and saw that Richard was sitting like a stone himself, eyes fixed on the boys and cup halfway to his mouth.

'Richard?' said David, 'are you okay? ... Richard!'

He nudged him and Richard came out of his trance.

'I remember,' he said, gazing at David with

glassy eyes. 'I know what happened the day of the accident.'

'Steady on,' said David. 'Are you sure you're all right. You've gone very pale.'

'Martin was skimming pebbles ... just like those boys ... then he picked up a big stone and slugged me.'

David raised his eyebrows. 'Are you absolutely certain?'

'Yes, of course I am,' snapped Richard. 'You don't think I'd make it up do you? I know we want to nail Martin, but there are limits.

'I must have been knocked out because the next thing I remember is swimming towards the rock where I was found.'

'But, Alison said you couldn't swim.'

'She assumed that because I choose not to swim now.' Richard explained about the swimathon he'd entered in his teens and shuddered. 'It's a good job I did learn though; otherwise we wouldn't be having this conversation. I'd have been a goner.'

'Sooo ... we now know Martin was definitely responsible for your accident.'

'Yes ... but it wasn't an accident, was it? ... Look, I doubt Alison told you the whole story of what happened that day. You see, I'm afraid I took a dislike to Martin right from the outset because I could tell he was itching to get his hands on Alison.'

David tried not to look shocked.

'Oh, sorry, David,' Richard chuckled, having recovered his good humour. 'I keep forgetting. That's not what you want to hear, is it?'

David smiled. 'Only because I don't like the thought of Alison and Martin together, any more than you do.'

'Anyway,' said Richard, 'I hired a boat and followed them. It was a stupid thing to do ... and I regretted it as soon as I crashed onto the beach.

'Then I sent Alison home after giving her a pretend message from Fay. I just wanted to tell Martin to butt out ... and he obviously decided to eliminate the opposition. He started skimming stones, but it never occurred to me he might use one as a weapon. Of course it's all circumstantial and Martin came up with a good cover story.'

David chewed his lower lip thoughtfully. 'On its own it would be difficult to prove ... but, perhaps with all the other incidents...?'

They strolled back to the flat and David fumbled for his car key as they entered the courtyard. 'Thanks for putting me up Richard ... and thanks for the meal last night. I really enjoyed my visit.'

'That's okay,' said Richard. 'Look on it as an apology for my bad manners. As I recall, I wasn't very polite to either you or Fay when I came down. I think I knew as soon as we got to Southcliffe that Alison and I were doomed. She was just so happy to be home and I knew it wouldn't be long before she'd want to move back again.'

'Well, at least you both found out before entering a disastrous marriage,' said David. 'And I'm glad you've regained your memory. The question is what to do about it.'

'Keep a close eye on Martin. Because I'm not sure we could make anything stick at the moment.'

'You're probably right. Let me know if you remember anything else.'

'I will,' said Richard.

It was early afternoon when David set the sat nav and started on the long journey home. The first thing he had to do was work out how much to tell Fay. He wouldn't be able to fob her off. She was far too shrewd ... and far too nosy.

***

As Richard waved David off, he was thinking about Alison's first fiancé's accident. He'd decided not to mention it because he didn't have a shred of evidence; only a feeling, which he recognised could have been created by his intense dislike of Martin.

CHAPTER 33

When David walked through the front door, he found a note from Fay propped up by the kettle.

'David, meet us at the hospital, when you get back. Reg has been taken ill. Love Fay x.'

Now what? David turned round and went out of the house.

***

At the hospital, David found Fay in the A&E waiting room, comforting Winnie who looked distraught. 'It's really not your fault,' she was saying. 'If anything, I'm probably to blame. I should have pointed out the dangers more clearly.' She turned as her husband came over. 'Oh, David, there you are.'

As she got up to hug him, he could see she was close to tears. She drew him down on the seat beside her, holding his hand tightly, while Winnie, crying quietly, screwed a handkerchief round in her fingers.

'Do try and stay calm,' said Fay. 'I'm so worried you'll make yourself poorly.'

'What's happened?' asked David.

'Winnie thinks it's all her fault because she

picked the wrong roots from the end of the garden to make horseradish sauce,' replied Fay.

'Hang on, love, you're not making any sense. What's this got to do with Reg being ill?'

'I'm sorry, David, I was forgetting you haven't heard ... don't you ever answer your mobile? I must have rung three or four times this afternoon.'

'Darling, you know I turn my phone off when I'm driving and the first thing I saw when I got home was your note so I came straight over. Just tell me what's going on.'

'Well, Reg has got aconite poisoning ... Winnie picked what she thought was horseradish from the overgrown area in their garden that backs onto the allotments. She wanted to make sauce to go with the beef she was cooking and she'd run out of the supermarket stuff.'

'How did she know it was horseradish? I wouldn't have thought Winnie would be into things like that. It's not like it's your everyday vegetable.'

'Well, that's the whole point,' Fay snapped waspishly. 'She didn't know. Neither did she know there was monkshood growing there as well. It looks similar and she dug that up that instead.

'The doctor said she was lucky not to have poisoned herself because even touching the root can be dangerous. Fortunately, she washed her hands after grating it and the doctor checked her over ... just in case ... but he said she was okay ... and luckily she doesn't like horseradish-'

'-Okay, okay ... I get the gist. But, what made her dig anything up? Why didn't she go to the shops and buy a jar? ... Or just do without?'

'I'm sure that's what she would have done if I hadn't pointed out they had it in the garden.' Fay scrabbled in her bag for a tissue and dabbed her eyes. 'I saw it ... just after they moved in ... and showed it to Alison and Martin. Winnie must have been there as well ... only come to think of it, I don't remember seeing her.'

David put his head in his hands. 'Oh, no!'

Fay touched her husband's arm. 'It'll be alright,' she said, in a small voice. 'Luckily, one of the paramedics suspected food poisoning and asked if Reg had eaten anything unusual.

'Winnie mentioned she'd made sauce from a plant in the garden so he brought it to the hospital and as soon as they knew what it was, they were able to treat him. He'll feel rough for a while, but they say he should be all right.'

A doctor emerged from the cubicle and came over. 'He's going to be fine,' he said. 'I've arranged for him to stay overnight ... just so we can keep an eye on him ... but he should be able to go home tomorrow.' He turned to Winnie. 'You can go in and see him now,' he added.

Winnie blew her nose. 'Will you wait here for me, Fay?'

'Yes, of course we will,' said Fay. 'Go see Reg

and give him our love.'

'I still don't understand,' said David as their friend walked away. 'You don't remember seeing Winnie when you pointed out the horseradish ... so how did she know about it?'

'I've no idea.' Fay shrugged. 'Perhaps she was there and I've forgotten. All I remember is walking round the garden with Alison and Martin. I also saw the monkshood and explained how it was toxic so you have to be careful not to mix them up. I even turned over a root of each to show them the difference.'

'You showed Martin a root of monkshood and told him it was poisonous?'

'Sounds like I'm being given the third degree here,' said Fay, 'but, yes, I did. I had no idea anyone would decide to make horseradish sauce ... who eats it anyway? ... and if they do, the supermarket's just down the road.'

She sighed. 'Despite that, I do feel responsible. If I hadn't been showing off my knowledge, none of this would have happened.'

'Are you sure you identified them the right way round?' David winced under the withering glare. 'Okay, you're sure ... incidentally, where are Alison and Martin? I'd have thought at least Alison would be here to look after Winnie.'

'I'm sure she would if she was around,' said Fay, 'but, she and Martin went off to do Christmas shopping. I was going to ring her, but decided to wait until I could say Reg was okay. No point in worrying her unnecessarily.'

Winnie left Reg's cubicle around half an hour later, looking happier. 'He's feeling better now,' she beamed, 'and must be on the mend because he's starting to complain about having to wait to go on to the ward.'

'Does he need anything?' asked David. 'I could collect some things if you like.'

'That's very kind, but the hospital can provide essentials for the night and he should be home in the morning. Besides, you've had a long drive and must be tired. Fay told me about your sudden flight to London.'

'Oh yes,' said Fay. 'We must talk about your long drive back from the city and what you've been doing over the weekend. I'd almost forgotten about that.'

'Yes, well, let's wait until we get home,' said David. 'Winnie, just one question; how did you know there was horseradish at the bottom of your garden?'

'Oh, I didn't,' said Winnie. 'Martin told me this morning.'

'Martin?' said Fay. 'Weren't you there when I pointed it out, just after you moved in?'

'No, I don't think so, dear. Alison and Martin popped in to see me before they went shopping. I was just putting a joint of beef in the oven and Alison had gone back to the annexe to pick up something she'd forgotten. I mentioned to Martin that I'd run out of horseradish sauce ... just to make conversation really ... and he told me we had some growing in the garden.

'He described exactly what it looked like and suggested I did some home-made sauce for Reg. I'd been going to pop out and buy a jar, but then I thought, why not have a go at making it? I found a recipe on the internet ... and discovered I had all the ingredients - even cream, because I'd brought some to go with our pudding - then I dug up what Martin said was horseradish and made the sauce.'

'How did Martin describe it?' Asked Fay.

'Well ... let me see ... he said to be sure not to mix it up with another plant as that was poisonous. He told me the one I wanted had a pointed brown root and to make sure I avoided the lighter ones. Then he explained where to find it ... and I made sure I only picked what he told me to.'

'Are you sure that's how Martin described it?' asked David.

'Oh yes,' said Winnie. 'I wrote it down as he said it, in case I forgot.'

'He told you the wrong way round,' said Fay. 'He gave instructions to pick the poisonous roots.'

David and Fay looked at each other.

'Well, that's one mystery solved,' said Fay. 'Martin mixed up the descriptions. An easy mistake I suppose, after all this time. Still, I wish he'd kept his mouth shut and then none of this would have happened.'

David said nothing. He'd just added another incident to the list and now it was time for action.

Later, after David had said goodbye to Fay who was getting ready to take Winnie home, he was about to head back to his own car when he saw a policeman talking to the consultant who'd been looking after Reg and went over to join them.

'Well, if that's all...?' The doctor was reaching for his pager and when the policeman nodded, he hurried off.

'Excuse me,' asked David. 'Are you here because of the poisoning?'

The policeman looked surprised. 'Yes, how, did you know?'

'An educated guess,' smiled David, gesturing towards the retreating physician. 'That doctor was looking after Reg, our friend ... and he's the one who was poisoned.'

'You make it sound like a crime's been committed,' commented the policeman, 'but, it's purely routine; we're always informed about cases involving poison ... just to rule out anything sinister ... but it looks like this was a genuine mistake.'

'I see. Well, what happens now?'

'Nothing, really; it'll go on record; but it might be an idea to make sure your friend's wife sorts out the difference between horseradish and monkshood for the future.'

'I doubt she'll be making that sauce again,' laughed David. '... Sorry, but I didn't catch your name.'

'I didn't say.' The policeman showed David his warrant card and looked at him shrewdly. 'I'm PC Mike Bolton. Is something worrying you?'

'No, no.' David wasn't quite ready to voice his concerns. 'I'm just glad Reg will be okay.'

'Well, he was lucky,' said Mike. 'If his wife hadn't called the ambulance when she did ... and if the paramedic hadn't been on the ball ... it could have been a different story.'

'Aconite poisoning can be fatal then?'

'Yes, if it's not treated properly ... and in time.'

'So Reg really was fortunate?'

'I'd say so.' Mike was edging towards the door. 'Well, goodnight, Sir.'

'Goodnight.'

David waved abstractedly and set off for the car park. PC Mike Bolton, he thought. I must remember that name.

CHAPTER 34

Fay was waiting for David when he arrived home a few minutes after her. 'You look done in,' she said, opening the fridge and taking out a bottle. 'Luckily I found some chilli in the freezer so we can eat in about half an hour.'

It was only then that David realised how was hungry he was. He'd stopped for a sandwich earlier, but that was five hours ago and breakfast was a distant memory.

'Why did you go over and talk to that policeman?' Fay handed him a generous measure of wine.

Relieved that she'd deferred her interrogation, David chinked glasses before taking a sip. 'No reason ... I just wondered why he was there. It seems they check on all cases of poisoning in case there's something sinister.'

'And you think there is something sinister, don't you?'

'What makes you say that?'

'Come on David, I've lived with you long enough to know when something's bothering you ... and you've been worried for a while now.' She took another sip from her glass. 'I bet I'm right in thinking it's why you went to see Richard ... and I bet I'm also right in saying it's to do with Martin.'

David stared. 'How did you know?'

'Well, it didn't take much brainpower.' Sinking down, Fay patted the sofa, inviting him to join her. 'You wouldn't have driven all that way if you weren't worried ... especially this time of year? And why else would you ask about Malcolm when I rang last night? Besides, Martin's the only person other than Alison with a connection to Richard and she never really explained why she left them both together on that beach last year ... also, we never got to the bottom of how Richard managed to fall in the sea on the way back ... nor do we really know why he went home so soon after.'

'Funnily enough, Richard opened up about that this morning,' David, who'd dropped down on the sofa beside his wife, explained how it was Richard's jealousy that made him follow them that afternoon. 'D'you remember Alison saying he didn't have a clue how he ended up in the water?'

Fay nodded.

'Well, he recovered his memory today in a very bizarre way and it seems it wasn't an accident after all.'

'It was Martin, wasn't it? ... And you also believe he was responsible for the horseradish misunderstanding.'

'Why would you think that?'

'Oh, David; when I said I'd shown Alison and Martin the different roots, you put your head in your hands and groaned.'

'I did not groan.'

'Well, you might just as well have done. ... Your face groaned.'

'I thought I had my head in my hands so how could you tell?'

'You know what I mean,' Fay leaned against David and sighed. 'Anyway, when I took Winnie back home, I found the piece of paper she'd written Martin's instructions on and brought it to show you.'

'Oh, good thinking,' David swallowed the last of his wine. 'Where is it? Let me see.'

Fay delved into her bag and they pored over the hand-written instructions that Winnie had got from Martin.

Poisonous root – cylindrical; yellow
Horseradish – pointed; dark brown

'The descriptions are the wrong way round,' said Fay, 'but, was it deliberate or genuine?'

'Oh, I'd say deliberate,' said David and over dinner he told Fay about everything he and Richard had discussed that weekend.

CHAPTER 35

Alison went from stall to stall, picking up bits and pieces in the Christmas market and for a while paid little attention as Martin lagged behind, deep in thought.

She knew he was sulking after seeing her on the phone to Ben earlier, but that was tough. There were people in her life other than Martin and he'd have to get used to it. She also knew he didn't enjoy shopping - few men did in her experience – and she wasn't surprised when he showed no interest in her purchases.

Eventually, even Alison was starting to flag and it was only when they stopped for coffee that she noticed how particularly distracted Martin was today. He barely responded to any of her conversation starters and she felt a pang of sympathy as they finished their drinks before posting the empty cups into a chute.

'Look, Martin,' she said, sharing out the shopping bags and linking their free arms. 'I know we're only half way through, but we don't have to do anymore now. There's plenty of time and we could come back another day ... or I could finish it myself. I don't mind.'

'No, it's okay, I'm fine.'

'But you're not, are you? You hate every minute and you really don't have to carry on if you don't want to. We could go home ... or do something else? ... What d'you think?'

Martin gazed over Alison's shoulder and frowned. 'Why don't we see what's on at the cinema,' he said. 'That'll give us a rest from the shopping and maybe we could do a bit more later on.'

'Okay,' Alison smiled. 'Actually, that's not a bad idea. Let's take the bags back to the car and get some lunch first.'

Waiting for the film to start, Martin was relieved to have found something other than shopping to keep them from going home. The bustle and flashing displays were giving him a headache and his thoughts were all over the place after this morning's disaster. Now, he desperately needed time and space to think about how to get out of the hole he had dug for himself.

Later, as Alison stared at the screen oblivious to everything except the implausible rom/com he'd steered her towards, Martin thought back to those few minutes when he'd been alone with Winnie in her kitchen.

Alison had decided that today would be Christmas shopping day and suggested popping in to see Winnie first, to see if she wanted anything while they were out. Then, she realised she'd forgotten a book of vouchers that had come through the door earlier that week.

'I'll just run and get them,' she'd said, jumping up as Reg put his head round the door to say he was off to buy a newspaper. He'd glanced over to Martin and the dislike was clear for all to see. Martin hated that look. It reminded him of his father.

While they were waiting for Alison to return, Winnie mentioned she'd run out of horseradish sauce. 'If I'd realised, I'd have asked Reg to get some,' she'd said, taking a joint of meat from the fridge and unwrapping it.

That was when Martin remembered Fay's botany lesson and the warning about poisonous roots. Horseradish is light in colour, she'd explained. Think of a monk's hood being dark and pointed and you can't go wrong.

What did go wrong, though, was that Martin had reversed the descriptions and Winnie had written them down word for word. If Reg fell ill, they'd say he should have offered to go and buy her a jar of sauce rather than take the risk of her making a mistake with the roots. He was usually so careful to stay out of the frame, but this time he'd done the opposite and there was no way out of it.

Winnie had seemed very keen to make the sauce and was looking for a recipe when Alison got back. He was sure she'd have gone straight into the garden to dig up the roots after they'd left.

Also, apart from leaving himself wide open to accusations, Martin was aware that he'd denied himself the experience of being there, which had been a big part of all the previous incidents.

Pushing his one time friend into the road had been the start of it. He could still feel the roughness of Tim's school blazer against his face as he pretended to trip against him.

He'd done it on impulse; and it had been such heady stuff for a teenager that he'd had to stop himself from punching the air in triumph.

But, even that didn't match up to the buzz he'd got from knocking Richard out last year. In fact the whole of that day had probably been one of the best he could remember; his love for Alison and hatred of Richard culminating in a mixture of terror and excitement as he tipped the new fiancé overboard.

Then, being suspected of attempted murder ... and later the realisation that Alison was back in his life ... had left him high on adrenaline. But, despite the drama, he'd hidden all trace of emotion and that had made everything feel even more intense.

Vandalising the car was pre-meditated, but it had been just as thrilling because every stab and scrape was delivered as if by proxy to Richard.

And setting the fire had made his heart thump so loudly he was worried they would hear it as he tiptoed past Reg and Winnie's sitting room door. His hands had been shaking as he turned on the gas and carefully arranged the flammable items knowing they could come in at any minute. The tide of relief that swept over him when he got away undiscovered had left him weak and shaky as he walked back to where Alison was waiting.

But, there'd been none of that today. He'd passed the power over to Winnie ... albeit without her knowledge. Forfeiting control meant that success, assuming he had been successful, would be a hollow victory – especially as he'd probably incriminated himself in the process.

Why hadn't he thought it through? Was he was nearing the end? Surely it was too soon, but perhaps destiny was catching up, just as he'd predicted it would.

Alison had been on her mobile when she came back with the vouchers. She'd just waved and blown Winnie a kiss while laughing down the phone to that student she shared lifts with.

He'd been getting more and more concerned about Ben. She behaved like a schoolgirl when she was talking to him and they were getting far too friendly. This was not how he'd imagined life with Alison would be.

***

It was getting dark when they came out from the cinema and the market looked festive with

Christmas lights flashing everywhere. Alison loved this time of year and skipped along to keep up with Martin's long strides. They did a bit more shopping and it was evening by the time Martin dropped her off.

She glanced over to Reg and Winnie's bungalow, which was in darkness as they got out of the car. 'That's strange,' she said. 'It's early for them to have gone to bed. I wonder if they're all right.'

'Why shouldn't they be?' Martin averted his eyes, '... and I remember now, Winnie said neither she nor Reg slept well yesterday so they were going to have an early night to make up for it.' As always, the lie tripped out smoothly.

'Oh, ... well, that probably explains it.' Alison took the last of her shopping out of the boot and slammed the lid shut.

'Careful,' said Martin. 'No need to crash it down like that.'

Alison laughed. 'It's just a car ... anyway, I'm shattered myself now so I'll pop in and see them before college tomorrow. Good idea about the cinema, I really enjoyed it.'

'I'm glad,' said Martin and kissed her. He'd had plenty of time in the cinema to work out his options and halfway down the path he turned abruptly and walked back.

'I'll always love you, Alison ... don't ever forget it.'

She smiled and his heart turned over.

"Course you will,' she laughed, 'and I'll always love you too. 'Night, Martin.' She reached up to give him another kiss.

Martin drove home slowly and found his mother waiting for him. Twenty minutes later, he went out again with his backpack containing a few toiletries and a change of clothes.

After throwing the luggage into the boot of his car, he closed it carefully and drove off into the night.

CHAPTER 36

'What are we going to do?' Fay's brow creased as she cleared the table after their meal.

David shrugged. 'I don't know. I've been trying to work it out all weekend. The problem is there's no evidence to link Martin to any of this...' He waved his hand over the piece of paper where Fay had listed everything in chronological order.

'What about the poisoning? We've got Martin's instructions written down.'

'But, in Winnie's handwriting. She could have mixed up what Martin said ... or Martin could say he made a mistake and we can't prove otherwise.' David thought for a moment. 'The only other option is Richard. I wonder if he'd be willing to repeat his allegations. It's not much, but it might be worth a try.'

'I'm going to ring Ruth,' said Fay. 'I've spoken to her a couple of times and she's always uneasy when Martin comes up in conversation. She might be able to tell us something.'

'Tread carefully, love, this is Martin's mum you're talking about and I doubt she'll say much, even if she does have concerns. You wouldn't, if it were Alison, would you?'

'No, I suppose not.' Fay hesitated. 'But I'll ring anyway to say what's happened. Then I'll ask her to tell Martin that Reg is going to be okay.'

'That'll annoy him,' chuckled David. 'He knows Reg doesn't like him, because he makes no secret of it.'

Fay dialled the number and, when Ruth answered, gave a brief explanation of what had happened.

'... Anyway, I'm just ringing to say Reg has been very ill, but he's all right now and will be discharged from hospital tomorrow,' she concluded, before adding, 'Would you pass that message on to Martin, please.'

'Yes, of course, 'whispered Ruth and immediately rang off.

'Well that was odd, even by her standards,' said Fay, replacing the receiver. 'You were right. She hardly said anything ... but I heard her gasp when I told her how Martin's mix up of instructions had been the reason for Reg to fall ill.

'Wouldn't you have thought she'd have wanted to know why he was telling Winnie stuff like that? It's obvious he'd not have any gardening knowledge. She truly is a peculiar person.'

David smiled at the indignant face. 'You're not really surprised are you? I said you'd get nothing out of her, but at least now she knows it could have been a lot more serious.'

'Serious? Don't you mean fatal? If Reg had died, Martin could be facing a manslaughter charge.'

'I doubt it. There's no real proof and a lawyer would get it thrown out in no time.'

David took the receiver from Fay and dialled Richard's number. A girl answered and passed the phone over when he said who he was.

'Hi, Richard, sorry to bother you, but I thought I'd update you on what's been happening.'

'Is Alison all right?'

'Yes, she's fine. It's Reg this time. You remember, I told you about Alison's landlord?' David described what had been occurring in Southcliffe while he was driving home. 'Now you've recovered your memory, I was wondering how you'd feel about telling the police what really happened on the day of your accident.'

There was a long pause.

'Well,' said Richard, 'it's not that I mind doing it, but I really don't see how it will make any difference ... especially after all this time. It'll be my word against Martin's and, much as I hate to admit it, his story sounds more rational. There was no motive. I'd only just met Martin and although I was engaged to Alison at the time, she broke it off the following week. She's also been with Martin ever since so why would he need to get rid of me if Alison was thinking of dumping me anyway?'

'Yes, you're probably right,' David noted the trace of regret in Richard's voice. 'It was just a thought.'

'We might have more luck if there was evidence to back it up. Anyway, let me know if anything else happens ... and watch out for Alison. I wouldn't put it past him to turn his attentions on her. She's very attractive and if he thinks she's flirting ... or being flirted with...'

Richard left the sentence hanging as David felt his stomach knot. Until then, the thought hadn't crossed his mind. He replaced the receiver and turned away so Fay wouldn't see his face. He couldn't lay that on her. There was no telling what she might do if she thought Alison was in danger.

***

Richard put the phone down and looked over to his latest girlfriend as she sprawled on the sofa, watching a movie on Netflix. She was just out of her teens and he, fast approaching thirty-five, was starting to notice the age gap.

Tonight, Sarah looked particularly young. She'd come back from her parents about an hour ago, taken a shower and was dressed for bed in a Minnie Mouse onesie. Her hair, still damp, fell across her face and she pushed it back impatiently so as not to miss any of the film.

'Is everything okay?' She asked, reaching for another chocolate without taking her eyes off the screen.

'Yes, fine.' The film was noisy and he wanted to think. 'I'll be in the kitchen making a drink,' he added.

A few minutes later Richard sat nursing the ***'My partner is called Miss Right ... her first name is Always'*** mug that Alison had given him after a particularly fiery argument. As a reminder, she'd said and that time it was he who'd lunged and started the wrestling match.

Sipping cautiously at scalding coffee, he took a long hard look at his life. There was no doubt he'd been successful, but he'd watched plenty of prosperous thirty-something's crash and burn and had no desire to join their number. He was in a young man's game and maybe he should quit while he was ahead.

These thoughts weren't new, but seeing David had made Richard realise he'd never really got over Alison. He knew he'd not treated her well - particularly during their visit to Southcliffe – and he didn't blame her for breaking the engagement. At the time he thought he'd soon forget her. But he'd been wrong.

It had also been a shock to suddenly regain his memory, especially now he knew for certain Martin had tried to kill him ... and when that hadn't worked, he'd come looking for him, perhaps meaning to have another go.

He felt a shiver run through him as he reflected on what might have happened had Martin targeted him instead of the car ... and what might still happen if Martin turned his attentions to Alison.

When Richard woke the following morning, he made a decision. Packing a few things, he told his girlfriend he was going away for couple of days.

Then he phoned the hotel in Southcliffe where he'd stayed before and booked a room. Alison may not want any more to do with him, but he'd never know for certain unless he gave it a try.

CHAPTER 37

Ruth replaced the receiver after Fay's call and knew she ought to alert someone; but all her energy had drained away during their conversation. A little while later though, the lethargy vanished when Martin walked through the door and his edginess confirmed her suspicions.

'I know you made that man ill today,' she shouted, her anger rising as she blocked his bid to escape upstairs. 'The same as I know you caused Alison's fiancé to nearly drown last year.'

Martin's glare made her shrink back, but she was determined to see it through. 'You didn't go camping the following week either, did you? You went to London and smashed up his car.'

Turning away, she missed the surprised drop of his jaw.

'Then there was that boy Tim ... and neither would I be surprised if you had something to do with Alison's first fiancé's accident.'

Ruth was panting now, having said far more than she'd intended, and the jolt of fear as he pushed past, made her gasp.

When she heard him moving around in his room she knew he would go and a few minutes later she watched from the window until the taillights disappeared. Although it was unforgivable, she hoped with all her heart he'd never come back.

***

Martin was in chaos as he loaded his car, aware that his mother was watching from the window. How did she know all those things? He'd been so careful. Was she psychic?

Putting these thoughts aside with difficulty, he knew he had to focus because there was one more thing to do before he drove away from Southcliffe forever.

Half an hour later he was on the road to London, his broad plan being to leave the car somewhere in a suburb. It would be far too conspicuous to drive around once they were on to him ... and he knew his mother would tell. Then he would catch a train and go somewhere as far away as possible.

He'd need money and it occurred to him that his cards would be stopped once the police were involved; so he pulled into the next service station and drew out the maximum from a cash machine. Then he refuelled and asked the man on the till for as much cashback as he would allow. If luck was on his side, he may have one more chance to draw from another ATM tomorrow.

Martin was on autopilot when he parked in a residential street in Richmond during the early hours.

After sleeping fitfully until daybreak, he put everything he could carry into a backpack and picked up his camping gear. He hated leaving the car, but it would give him away so, reluctantly, he locked it and headed for the station, stopping at another cash point on the way.

Aware now that he was hungry, he went into a café for breakfast before catching a train from Richmond to London.

Victoria Station was quiet as he scanned the departure board and noticed how one destination stood out from all the others.

After navigating through a touch screen machine, he waited for delivery of the single ticket and checked the platform number again.

The train would leave in fifteen minutes.

CHAPTER 38

Alison had overslept and was only just ready when Ben knocked for her the next day. It was her turn to drive so he'd parked his car further up the road and was ready to go.

She had intended to check on Reg and Winnie, but there was no time now. In any case, Winnie had just pulled back the front room curtains and blown her a kiss.

'They're obviously okay then,' Alison waved before getting into the car and opening the door for Ben.

'Who's okay?'

'My neighbours,' said Alison. 'No worries,' she added when Ben gave her a quizzical look. 'There's no reason why they shouldn't be.'

'Good weekend?'

'Not bad, I suppose.' Alison stifled a yawn. 'Martin and I did some Christmas shopping yesterday ... then we went to the cinema. I think that's why I'm so tired ... and I've not had breakfast.'

'Do you want to stop and have some now?'

'No, it'll make us late. I'll be okay. I've grabbed a few biscuits to keep me going.' She pulled out of the drive into the road.

'Did you manage that assignment last week? I finished mine yesterday and am quite pleased with it. Hope it gets a good mark.'

Alison shot a glance at her passenger and smiled at the smugness. 'Oh, you're way ahead of me. I've barely looked at it. I can see you're going to be one of those annoying students ... always out in front.'

Approaching the brow of the hill that led into town, Alison's foot moved to the brake, but when she pressed nothing happened.

'Omigod!'

'What's wrong,' Ben was gripping the dashboard. 'You're going too fast. For God's sake, slow down.'

'I can't, I can't!' The car picked up speed. 'The brakes won't work ... omigod! ... what's going on?'

'Use the handbrake.'

Still pumping the brake pedal, Alison was approaching a turn in the road far too quickly as she and Ben tried to pull up the handbrake. But it was too late. The car slewed round and the passenger side hit a tree as they mounted the pavement.

Alison opened her eyes, slowly. One minute she'd been driving to college, the next, she was sure she was going to die. What the hell was going on?

A driver coming from the opposite direction had stopped and got out of his van. 'Are you all right?' He asked, running over to Alison.

'I think so.' Aware that her neck was hurting, Alison's voice shook as she looked over to where Ben was sitting, unconscious and trapped in his seat by crumpled wreckage. Her hand flew to her mouth. 'Oh, no ... Ben? ... Ben? ... Are you okay?'

She turned back to the man still standing at the window, her eyes wide. 'What happened? Why didn't the brakes work?'

'I don't know. But it explains why you were going so fast,' said the man. 'Look, I've phoned for both police and ambulance so someone should be here soon.'

As he spoke, they heard sirens approaching and a moment later, an ambulance pulled up in front of the car.

The driver ran over to assess the situation and, seeing that cutters would be needed, asked the police officer who had just parked opposite to call the fire service. After checking Alison over, he fitted her with a neck brace and took her to the ambulance while the other medic slid into the driver's seat and gave Ben what help she could while they waited.

'The fire brigade is on its way ... How's the passenger?' After making his call, the policeman had gone over to the wrecked car and the medic shook her head.

'Not good. He's got internal injuries and his legs are trapped. We won't know how bad it is until we get him out.'

Now settled in the ambulance, Alison asked the driver if he would fetch her bag from the back seat of the car. 'D'you think he'll be all right?' she asked when he came back. 'If only that tree hadn't been there.'

'I'm afraid his side of the car is pretty smashed up, but they'll know more once they get him free.'

Soon after, the fire engine arrived and when the sound of metal cutting started, the other medic returned to the ambulance. 'They reckon it'll take about twenty minutes,' she said and, turning to Alison, asked, 'Are you okay to wait so we can take you to the hospital together?'

'Yes, of course,' said Alison. 'It's the least I can do. I feel so responsible, but it really wasn't my fault. The brakes just weren't there.' She ran a finger between her neck and the brace as her eyes filled with tears. 'When will I be able to get this thing off?'

'It's just a precaution,' said the driver. 'They'll check you again at the hospital and maybe do an X-ray. My guess is, you're probably okay, but better safe than sorry.'

'Can I make a phone call?'

'Yes, of course,' said the other medic before going back to her patient.

The policeman came over to the ambulance just as Alison switched off her phone. 'I'm PC Mike Bolton,' he said. 'I take it you were driving. Do you know what caused the accident?'

'Not really,' said Alison. 'Only that I went to brake and nothing happened ... I kept trying ... then Ben and I pulled the hand brake up, but we were going too fast...'

'I see,' said Mike. 'I have to ask I'm afraid, but did you drink any alcohol last night ... or this morning?'

'No.'

'Are you up to doing a breathalyser test?'

'I think so.'

Alison was thankful she had nothing to worry about and Mike logged the negative result in his notebook. 'I'll need to see your documents,' he said. 'When was the car last serviced?'

'A couple of months ago; my boyfriend's a mechanic and he looks after my car. I've never had problems before. The brakes were non-existent.' This time the tears spilled over.

'I think that's enough for the moment.' The ambulance driver intervened. 'She's in shock ... and anyway, it looks like the other one's free now.'

He ran to help get Ben onto a stretcher and his colleague monitored the unconscious student all the way to the hospital.

When they reached A & E, a team of medics whisked Ben away while Alison was taken to a cubicle to wait for the next available doctor.

A few minutes later, Fay rushed in after her second dash to the hospital inside twenty-four hours. She'd called David, to let him know what had happened and he was also on his way.

Alison took one look at her mother and burst out crying as Fay went over and hugged her.

'Whatever happened?' Fay was close to tears herself. 'Are you all right?'

'Yes, I'm okay,' sniffed Alison. 'Only, I wish they'd take this brace off.'

Just then, the doctor came in and Fay was ushered back to the waiting room, still not knowing the full story. But at least Alison was in one piece.

As Fay went to sit down, she saw David coming through the door and beckoned him over.

'How is she?' His voice was sharp with worry. 'What's been going on?'

'The doctor's with her now. I saw her briefly and she looked all right ... but, we'll have to wait until he's finished before we can find out more.'

David bought them both a cup of coffee and while they were drinking it, he saw PC Mike Bolton arrive.

Mike also recognised David and came over. 'Hello, again,' he said. 'What are you doing here? Did your friend take a turn for the worse?'

'No, it's our daughter this time. She's been involved in a car accident and we're waiting to see her. She's being checked over at the moment.'

'Is her name Alison Albright?' Asked Mike.

'Yes,' David jumped up. 'How did you know?'

'I was called to the scene,' said Mike. 'I also

need to speak to your daughter again, when the doctor is through.'

'What exactly happened? All we know is she was hurt and brought here by ambulance.'

'Yes, that's right and this morning it all seemed straightforward. The driver - your daughter - lost control of the car as she came down a hill. She said the brakes wouldn't work and the car swerved off the road, colliding with a tree.'

Fay shuddered.

'She was fortunate,' said Mike, 'but the passenger wasn't so lucky and I believe he's in intensive care.'

'That must be the student Alison's been talking about,' said Fay, her voice high with anxiety. 'How awful; does Alison know how badly hurt he is?'

'She's got a pretty good idea,' said Mike. 'She was there when the fire fighters were cutting him out of the wreckage.'

'Poor Alison,' whispered Fay. 'Something must have happened. She's usually such a good driver.'

'Well, that's why I need to talk to her again,' said Mike. 'One fire officer stripped the bonnet away in order to free her friend and noticed the brakes appeared to be damaged even though they weren't in the area that had been smashed up.

'We're arranging for the car to be inspected,

but if he was right...?'

Fay and David looked at each other with mounting horror.

'I gather Ms Albright's boyfriend maintains her car and that it was serviced a couple of months ago. I need to get hold of his details so I can have a word. Perhaps you could tell me who he is - and where he lives - to save me bothering her again?'

'Yes, I can do that,' said David. 'Here, give me your notebook and I'll write it down.'

Fay looked at her watch. 'I'll have to go and get Reg soon,' she said. 'I promised Winnie I'd pick him up and take him home this morning.'

'The guy with the aconite poisoning?'

'Yes, that's right,' said Fay. 'Reg is Alison's landlord. How did you know?'

'Oh, I was here yesterday. Mr Albright came over and spoke to me. I think you were just leaving to take the man's wife home. Your husband, as I recall, seemed rather worried about something.'

Mike turned to David. 'Hmm ... One case of poisoning and one suspicious car accident ... both have a connection to Ms Albright and both happened in the space of twenty-four hours. That's a bit of a coincidence.' Mike continued to stare. 'Do you think they may be related?'

'As a matter of fact, I do,' said David. 'Look, I need to talk to you about this. Could we meet up later? You also need to speak to Reg, but he's probably still groggy after yesterday and won't be up to going to the police station. Is there any chance you could meet us at his house?'

Mike hesitated.

'It's really important you hear what we have to say,' said David. 'Because I think Alison's boyfriend, might be responsible in both cases.'

'Okay,' said Mike, glancing at the name David had written down for him, 'I'll be round in a couple of hours. But, first I need to talk to this Martin Landon and see what he has to say for himself.'

'Well, he's probably at work now,' said David. 'He's a manager in the last garage you pass, as you leave town. Give me your notebook again and I'll write down Reg and Winnie's address.'

'Thanks ... see you later then.' Mike turned to go.

Fay and David watched until he was out of sight.

'Surely Martin didn't do that,' Fay, dropped into a chair before her legs could give way. 'Maybe all the other things ... but he adores Alison and wouldn't harm her.'

'Yesterday, Richard said to keep an eye on Alison.' David took his wife's hand as he sat down beside her. 'He believes Martin would be capable of turning his attentions on her if he thought she was getting too friendly with someone else. Perhaps he doesn't like the fact she shares the drive to college with a young student.'

Fay's jaw dropped. 'Oh my goodness, you're right. I remember Alison saying how much Martin hates the set-up she has with Ben. Apparently he offered to drive Alison, just to stop her car sharing.'

'It all fits,' said David. 'And the sooner we tell Mike Bolton, the better. I'll go and get Reg. He needs to be in on this so that he can explain about the fire in his kitchen. You stay here and wait for Alison.'

'Someone will have to tell her about Martin, won't they,' said Fay. 'I suppose that'll be me, then?'

'Alison's not going to like it, whoever tells her,' said David. 'I'll speak to her later, if you prefer.'

'No, I'll do it. Poor Alison; she really doesn't have much luck with her men, does she? First Paul, then Richard ... and now Martin.'

'Yes, well Paul and Martin are definitely off the scene, but you never know, we may not have seen the last of Richard yet.'

***

While David and Fay were having their conversation, Richard was booking into the hotel in Southcliffe. He guessed David would be working, but decided to send a text to let him know he was here and suggest they meet up later.

Maybe he'd get a chance to see Alison as well,

but this time he must try not to mess it up.

***

David heard the ping on his phone as he walked Reg slowly to the car. Not many people sent him texts ... only the server and occasionally Fay or Alison ... so as soon as he'd settled Reg in the passenger seat, he pulled up the message, eyes widening when he saw who it was from.

He'd forgotten they'd exchanged mobile numbers yesterday and, when he read that Richard was in Southcliffe, he rang straight away to fill him in with the morning's events. 'This is a bit of luck,' he added. 'Now you can tell Mike Bolton your story as well.'

He gave the address – much to Reg's bewilderment - and told him to be there in a couple of hours.

David brought Reg up to speed as they drove back to his bungalow and he reluctantly agreed to tell Mike about Martin's suspicious behaviour after the fire.

'It's only my impression, mind,' said Reg when David explained what they were trying to do. 'I've no evidence.'

'I know that,' said David. 'We've none of us got any evidence, but, if Bolton's half the policeman I think he is, he'll take note of all the co-incidences and pull everything together. It's possible Martin over reached himself by tampering with Alison's car. Having serviced it recently, he's going to find it difficult to explain the faulty brakes.'

'But, will he?' argued Reg. 'Alison's car was parked outside so anyone could have done it.'

'Yes, but why would they?' David's testiness was thinly veiled as he tried not to think about how Martin could still worm his way out of everything.

Reg had been shocked at David's tone. He'd never heard him speak so sharply and could only imagine the anguish he was going through. He decided then to be as forceful and positive as he could when this PC Bolton arrived later that day.

CHAPTER 39

Ruth ignored the knock on the door. She couldn't face anyone this morning. Perhaps if she stayed out of sight and kept quiet, whoever it was would go away.

The next knock was louder and more insistent so she risked a peek from behind the curtains of the front bedroom window and saw a young policeman walking towards her neighbour ... the one who'd seen her earlier and waved. It was clear she was telling him all about it and as she watched, the policeman turned back to the house.

'Mrs. Landon,' he called through the letter-box. 'I know you're in. This is the police. Would you please open the door?'

Ruth sighed and went downstairs to let the officer in.

'I'm PC Bolton, said Mike, 'and I'm looking for Martin Landon ... your son, I believe.'

'He's working.'

'No, he's not,' said Mike. 'I went to the garage, but he's not been in. Is he here?'

'No, he isn't.'

'When did you last see him?'

Ruth thought for a moment. She had no

idea where Martin was but, if she explained how he took off last night, perhaps this Bolton man would leave her alone.

'He came home yesterday evening around nine and left very soon after ... and, before you ask, I don't know where he went.'

Mike sensed from the outset that Ruth wasn't telling him everything, but it was clear Martin had flown and therefore would need money. In fact, he may already have made a withdrawal and, if so, the bank would be able to pinpoint the location.

'Do you have your son's banking details?'

'No, but there's paperwork in his room.' Ruth led the way upstairs and took a fat folder from the desk drawer, which she handed to Mike.

'No online banking then?' Mike flicked through the statements, filed neatly in chronological order, which went back some five years, 'unusual for someone his age.'

Ruth shrugged. 'He's got an ipad so maybe he does that as well.'

Mike glanced at some of the pages and noticed a monthly direct debit - the only one Martin had set up – and pointed it out to Ruth. 'Do you know anything about this?'

Ruth shook her head. 'I've told you, I don't have anything to do with Martin's finances. He pays me housekeeping in cash and what he does with the rest of his money is none of my business.'

Mike made a note of the account details and got onto the station. 'I need someone to put the brakes on a bankcard,' he told the duty officer who answered, and read out the name, account number and sort code.

'And while they're on to the bank, would they check to see if he's drawn out any money over the last twenty four hours. If so, where did he get it from?

Oh, and one more thing; would they also get the details of a monthly direct debit. There's only one, but I'd like to know who he makes the payment to. It started nearly four years ago and is unlikely to be significant, but you never know...'

Mike switched his phone off and turned back to Ruth. 'Does it look like Martin's taken much with him?'

Ruth twitched her shoulders again. 'It's difficult to say. He does his own cleaning so I have no reason to come in here. The washing basket is in the bathroom and I leave his laundry outside the door when it's ready.'

'I see. Well, let me know if Martin comes back or if he gets in touch.'

He gave Ruth a contact number and, as he walked to his car, realised she'd not once asked why he wanted to speak to her son. Neither had she seemed surprised to see him. Something definitely wasn't right.

Mike looked at his watch. He was looking forward to meeting up with David Albright. Perhaps he would shed light on what was turning out to be a fascinating case.

CHAPTER 40

Fay had to wait another twenty minutes before Alison emerged from the cubicle, rubbing her neck with one hand and holding a foam support in the other.

'What did the doctor say?'

'It's whiplash and I have a few bruises, but other than that I'm okay and can go home. He told me to take paracetamol and this is just in case I need it,' she connected the velcro fastenings of the collar and carried it in a loop.

'Well, you were lucky. It could have been a lot worse,' said Fay.

'Yes, I know,' Alison paused. 'How's Ben?'

'I don't know, darling. All we know is that he's in intensive care.'

Alison's face fell. 'Oh, is he still that bad? ... And it's all down to me. If I hadn't been driving, none of this would have happened.'

'I don't think it's quite that simple,' said Fay, carefully. 'Look, why don't you come back with me and stay for a bit. You could even sleep in your old room tonight, if you like.'

'No, Mum, it's really not necessary. I'll be fine.'

'Yes, love, I'm sure you will, but indulge me

for once. I'd like to look after you ... if you'll let me.'

Alison hesitated.

'We could start with something to eat. You must be hungry. It's coming up to lunchtime and I've got home-made soup and bread at home, which I can get ready in no time.'

Alison realised she was starving now, having missed both breakfast and the biscuits she'd brought to keep her going. 'Okay,' she said. 'You win.'

After driving home, Fay bustled round preparing lunch while stealing glances at her daughter, who sat hunched over the kitchen table, her face drawn.

Later, having decided to wait until they'd eaten before saying anything, she settled Alison on the sofa with a blanket and took the chair opposite. 'Look, love, I know this is going to come as a shock, but it seems likely someone tampered with the brakes of your car.'

'What!' Alison gasped. 'I don't believe it. Who would do such a thing?'

'Well ... you're not going to like this...'

'Go on.'

'At the moment, the finger seems to be pointing at Martin.'

Alison slumped further into the cushions and winced in pain. 'Why has everyone got it in for Martin?'

Noting that Alison didn't seem as shocked as she should have been, Fay went over to the bureau and took out the list she and David had put together the previous evening. 'I'm afraid your dad and I also think Martin was involved in these incidents as well,' she said, thrusting the page into her daughter's hand.

The remaining colour drained from Alison's face when she saw what had been written. 'But, this is complete nonsense,' she shouted. 'Tim Burgess? ... Who the hell's Tim Burgess?' She flicked the paper with the back of her hand as if to brush away the lies.

'Have you been talking to Richard?' She yelled, reading the bit about his accident and the vandalised car ... 'And the fire? For heaven's sake, we were at the theatre that night. How could he have done that? ... And what's this about Reg...?'

Here she stopped and stared at her mother. 'Reg? ... poisoned?' she whispered. 'I had no idea. When did this happen?'

Fay told Alison about the horseradish mix up. 'You were shopping and we didn't want to worry you. That's why we didn't ring,' she explained. 'And then this morning's events took over in the drama stakes.

'Look, I know it's hard to imagine Martin sabotaging your car, but when you see all the other things that have happened when he's been around ...,' Fay gestured to the list still clutched in Alison's hand, '... well, we decided it was time to tell someone.'

'Oh yes. And when were you going to get round to telling me?'

'It's not like that, love,' said Fay quietly. 'We really only pieced it together last night and I doubt we'd have done anything if you hadn't had that accident. But, if Martin did disable your brakes, he's far too dangerous to be allowed to stay on the loose.'

'But, how do you know it was him?' persisted Alison. 'It could have been anyone.'

'Like who? You told me how suspicious Martin was when you started car-sharing with Ben. Jealousy can make people do strange things - even if there's a risk of hurting someone they love - and besides, who else but you and Martin have access to your car.'

Fay went to sit beside Alison and put an arm round her, squeezing her shoulders. 'That's why your dad has arranged to talk to the police round at Reg and Winnie's this afternoon.'

Alison shrank into her mother's arms and Fay's heart went out to her. 'Try and rest now,' she said. 'I know it's hard to believe ... and there was no easy way to tell you. I'll bring you a hot drink a bit later on.'

Fay gave her daughter a kiss before settling her down so she could sleep if she wanted to. Glancing at her watch, she left the room while wondering how David was getting on, a few minutes away at Reg and Winnie's house.

Alison could hardly summon up the energy needed to reach for the foam collar and wrap it round her neck. Exhausted, she closed her eyes. It was too ridiculous. How could Martin be responsible? It just wasn't possible.

But, even she couldn't block the nagging voice in her head that told her the only person to have a spare key to her car was Martin ... and why hadn't he responded to the message she'd left earlier, saying she was waiting to be taken to hospital after being hurt in a car accident?

CHAPTER 41

Sitting beside a window in the empty compartment, a sudden tightening in his stomach reminded Martin that he was nearing his destination. Perhaps it would be all right and a miracle would happen to wipe out the last two days; but, that was the stuff of fairy stories and could never happen.

It would probably all be over by now. Alison had said it was her turn to drive today and he wondered what the outcome had been. He hoped it was quick ... quicker than Paul.

Maybe he should have done something different, but there'd been no time and he loved Alison far too much to share her. He'd tried so hard to keep her close, but lately she'd started to slip away and he couldn't allow that to happen ... not now Ben was on the scene ... and if not Ben, someone else.

Then, there was his mother and he marvelled again at how she'd known all those things. He was glad he'd never have to face her again.

The rhythm of the train was hypnotic and Martin fell into an uneasy sleep. He dreamed he was running ... running from a raging fire as fast as he could, but he wasn't getting anywhere and flames were licking at his heels. He could feel the heat on his face as he looked back at the blaze.

Then the dream changed and he was driving, still trying to escape from some unknown terror. He stamped on the accelerator before changing to the brake pedal at the top of a steep hill. But, no matter how hard he pressed, the car wouldn't slow down. Martin opened his mouth in a soundless scream as he flew up in the air and hovered before plunging down again ... but, instead of the ground, an angry sea was boiling below ... waiting to smash him to pieces on the rocks.

Martin woke with a start and when he put a quivering hand to his face he found it was wet with tears. He wiped them away as an announcement informed passengers they would be arriving at the terminal shortly. 'Please make sure you take all your belongings and mind the gap as you leave the train,' the voice went on, but Martin had stopped listening.

His new life stretched out like a void; the old one gone forever.

CHAPTER 42

Mike's phone rang, just as he arrived at Reg and Winnie's bungalow.

'Hi Mike. Just to let you know the bank has stopped Landon's cards. He's drawn out two maximums ... one, yesterday from an M3 service station and the other, this morning, from an ATM in Richmond.'

'Thanks,' said Mike, 'Any news on the direct debit?'

'Yes, it's monthly rental for a lock-up about thirty miles away. The man who hires it out said Landon took it on three or four years ago, but he never sees him ... in fact he doesn't think he's ever been back. He said it's a bit of a mystery as it's not cheap. I've got the phone number. Do you want me to check it out?'

'No thanks,' said Mike. 'Give me the details and I'll look into it later.'

As he walked up the path to Reg and Winnie's bungalow, Mike sensed he was in for an interesting afternoon.

David showed Mike into the small sitting room where Reg was propped up on the sofa with pillows and a blanket. He looked frail and Winnie was sitting next to him, protectively.

Reg managed to raise a smile when David did the introductions and Richard, seated in an armchair, also waved an acknowledgement.

'Don't I know you?' Mike's eyebrows lifted when he heard Richard's name.

'I wouldn't have thought so,' said Richard, 'unless ... yes, you're the police officer I spoke to after my accident last year. You came and saw me at the hospital.'

'I remember,' said Mike. 'You'd fallen in the sea, looking for seals.'

'Well ... that's not actually what happened,' said Richard. 'You see, it wasn't an accident-'

'-Hold on, we're getting ahead of ourselves,' David was beginning to feel like the TV detective who calls everyone together at the end of each episode to reveal the murderer.

'PC Bolton, I asked you to come and see us this afternoon because I've been getting increasingly concerned about Martin Landon.'

He handed Mike a sheet of paper with brief descriptions of all the incidents and consulted the note he'd made for himself:

> *Tim Burgess - pushed under a car*
> *Richard - accident at sea*
> *Richard - car vandalised*
> *Reg & Winnie - kitchen fire*
> *Reg - aconite poisoning*

'We think Martin is responsible for all of

this,' he said and went through the list, describing each incident in detail.

Mike made notes and, when they'd all given their versions, told them what he'd found out from his recent phone call.

'I'm sorry to have to tell you,' he concluded, 'but Landon didn't turn up at the garage this morning and could be anywhere, by now.'

He paused as he thought back to his visit to Martin's workplace.

***

'Is Martin Landon here?' he'd asked, after locating two mechanics in the workshop.

'No,' a cocky young lad grinned mischievously. 'Why, what's he done?'

'Why do you assume he's done anything?'

'Well, that's usually why you lot come round, isn't it?'

'Yeah, that's right, Josh,' said an older man, popping up from behind a Volvo, 'especially for people like Landon.'

'Not all my visits are to do with crime,' said Mike and, as neither of them had seemed surprised that a policeman was asking about Martin, added, 'so ... what *is* he like?'

Josh and the other man stopped smiling.

'What do you mean?' Josh looked wary. 'We don't know him that well, do we Ron?'

'Well, what's his job here then?'

'Senior mechanic,' said Ron.

'And he takes advantage,' added Josh bitterly.

'In what way?'

'Well ... 'Josh hesitated and looked at Ron.

'What he means is Landon takes on all the good jobs and leaves the rubbish to us,' said Ron. 'You'll never see Landon under the bonnet of anything other than a top-notch car.'

'Yeah, that's right,' Josh kicked at a car tyre. 'It's not fair. He does all the test drives ... can't afford an expensive car, but he customised his own during working hours while we had to do all the work.'

'What car does he drive?' asked Mike, 'Write down the registration number and a brief description, please.' He handed his notebook and pen to Ron, who wrote in laborious capitals.

'What's he like as a person?' Mike took back the notebook and squinted at the barely legible writing.

Josh and Ron looked at each other again.

'If you ask me, he's spooky,' said Josh, at last.

'Yeah, that just about describes him,' added Ron.

Mike was starting to find this double act tiresome. 'What does he do or say to make you think he's spooky?'

'Well, that's just it,' said Ron, serious now. 'He doesn't really do or say anything. He's a young man in his twenties, but he never laughs or jokes with the rest of us. Most of the time, he doesn't speak at all, except to give his orders.'

'Yeah,' said Josh, 'he likes to give his orders all right. Mind you, I think he's got a girlfriend; must be his good looks that attract her though - unless he's different away from work.'

'His girlfriend's gorgeous,' commented Ron. 'I saw her once when she came to meet him. He must have something, but whatever it is he keeps it well hidden while he's here.'

'I see,' said Mike as Ron nudged Josh and they burst out laughing. 'Well, you've both been very helpful. Were you expecting him in this morning?'

'Oh yes,' said Ron. 'I'm working on the vehicle he was going to repair. Actually, it's not like him to stay away. He loves his cars and rarely takes time off.'

Mike wrote down his mobile number and gave it to Ron. 'If he shows up, give me a ring ... but don't tell him who you're calling.'

Ron and Josh exchanged glances.

'So he has done something then,' said Ron. 'Well, I'm not surprised. Sometimes he looks at you in a very strange way ... especially if you're telling him something he doesn't want to hear.'

'Don't jump to conclusions.'

Mike turned to leave. He found it telling that throughout the whole conversation, neither colleague had said one positive thing about Martin Landon, other than that he was good-looking.

***

Mike passed on the essence of what he'd found out from the garage and his subsequent conversation with Ruth Landon.

'Martin's colleagues pretty much summed him up in the same way you did,' he said. 'And it was interesting that when one said he was spooky, the other agreed.'

'Spooky?' David frowned. 'Maybe they're a bit scared of him.'

'Possibly,' said Mike. 'They didn't seem to have much in common with him ... neither did they seem surprised to see me ... and both assumed he'd done something wrong ... same as Mrs Landon. She never once asked why I wanted to see her son.

'We know he was in Richmond this morning and I've asked the local police to keep an eye open for his car. It's customised apparently - so I'd imagine it's quite conspicuous.'

'Yes, it is,' said David. 'He won't be driving it around for long if he wants to keep a low profile.'

Mike's mobile rang and he excused himself to take the call in the kitchen. When he returned, he had more news. Martin's car had been found and someone had definitely tampered with Alison's brakes.

'This means Landon could be facing an attempted murder charge when we find him,' said Mike. 'But, we need hard evidence before we have any hope of securing a conviction.'

As Mike was preparing to leave, it occurred to

Richard that maybe there was something in his theory about Paul's accident after all.

'Just one more thing,' he said. 'It might be nothing, but I've a hunch Martin may also have been responsible for Alison's first fiancé's death.'

Richard enjoyed the stunned silence.

'Whoa,' said David.. 'That's something I never thought of pinning on him. Where did you get that idea from?'

Richard explained how, despite Martin's aversion to 'un-cool' cars, Alison had seen him driving an old Skoda on the afternoon Paul was knocked down. 'On the day of my so-called 'accident' I confronted Martin and accused him of staging a 'hit-and-run.' I wasn't really sure, but the colour drained out of his face and he looked like he'd been hit with a sledgehammer.'

'What did he say?' David sounded sceptical.

'Just that he'd been taking the car to be crushed; but why would he remember that sort of detail two years later, if it wasn't significant? I think he knew he'd given himself away and I'm sure that's why he tried to kill me.

'Of course it's all circumstantial ... and Martin got everyone to believe I'd been looking for seals...'

Ignoring the sarcasm, Mike made another note. 'I'll check it out,' he said, 'but it does sound a bit tenuous.'

'Yes, I know,' Richard glared at the policeman. 'But I was there and I saw Martin's reaction

… Besides, why else would he hit me? I said at the time he was jealous … but I suppose that sounds 'tenuous' as well' he added irritably.

'Is that what you were going to tell me in the police station last year?' asked Mike.

'Yes it was. But, I knew I didn't have a hope in hell of convincing anyone, so I didn't bother.'

Mike snapped his notebook shut and stood up. He had a plan now. Walking back to the car, he took out his mobile and punched in the number his colleague had given him earlier.

CHAPTER 43

It was David who got up to see Mike to the front door; Reg was looking tired and he could see Winnie was anxious and wanted him to rest.

'Come on, Richard,' he said, 'let's leave Reg in peace. It's my turn to treat you to something to eat although it won't be as good as the meal we had on Saturday.'

Ten minutes later, seated in a café overlooking the sea, Richard wondered out loud how Alison was. He'd been shocked when David told him about the crash, but the meeting with Mike Bolton had taken his mind off it.

'Yes, I was thinking about that as well,' said David. 'I was going to take you to see her, but perhaps I'd better check with Fay first. I haven't had a chance to tell either of them that you're here.'

He took out his phone and selected the number.

'Oh, hi,' said Fay, 'how did you get on; did you manage to convince that policeman?'

'I think so,' said David. 'Actually, I had a bit of help. Richard's here and joined us for the meeting.'

The line went quiet.

'He came because he was worried about Alison,' continued David. 'It was a gut feeling, which proved to be right and he's booked in at the hotel. The thing is, do you think Alison would like to see him?'

'When?'

'I don't know ... now, I suppose.'

'Wait there, I'll go and see.' Fay came back a couple of minutes later. 'She's sleeping at the moment and I think we should give her some warning; maybe tomorrow?'

'Okay,' said David, 'you're probably right. I'll tell Richard. See you soon.'

Richard was disappointed, but could see Fay's point.

'I'll ring in the morning to let you know how she is,' said David and, while Richard went back to his hotel room, he set off home. It had been an eventful few days and he was feeling weary. He would be glad now when life got back to normal.

***

A man was waiting when Mike arrived and he opened the door of the lock-up as the police officer got out of the car.

Unsure of what they'd find, Mike took a deep breath and walked in with the owner who fumbled for the light switch. In front of them was the shape of a car covered in tarpaulin and, when Mike pulled the covering away, they saw it was a green Skoda.

The man moved forward and Mike caught his arm. 'Don't touch anything,' he warned, catching sight of damage to the wing that could have been caused by hitting an object or person at speed.

'Why's he paying good money to keep this heap of old junk?' The owner scratched his head. 'It doesn't make sense.'

'Not on the face of it,' agreed Mike, 'but we've made quite a find here and there may still be viable forensic evidence.'

He locked the garage door and kept the key, telling the owner not to let anyone in. Then he went back to the police station where he tracked down his sergeant and told him everything he'd found out, finishing with the information about the Skoda in the lock-up.

'Good work, Mike,' said the sergeant. 'I'll get on to forensics first thing to see if it's the car that was involved in the 'hit and run.' The question is where did Landon go once he left Richmond?'

'Could have gone anywhere; maybe he headed for a mainline station in London ... or an airport ... then he'd have been spoiled for choice.'

'You're right,' said the sergeant. 'We must get a description out. He's clearly unstable and we don't have a clue where to start looking for him.'

He frowned as an idea came to him. 'I know one of the TV news editors ... met him when he came down with his team after that body was found in a quarry a couple of months ago. ... He said he used to live round here and played on the site as a child.

'Perhaps he would arrange for a mention on 'News at Ten.' Maybe someone will remember Landon if they see a picture on TV.'

Mike left the sergeant to his phone calls and thought back to the arrogant Londoner who'd been fished out of the sea by the lifeboat crew and who wanted to press charges against Landon. He also remembered the niggle at the back of his mind as he'd left the police station that day ... a feeling that something wasn't stacking up.

It was good to know his instinct had been proved right. Moments like this made him glad he was a policeman and he headed home knowing it had been a particularly productive day.

CHAPTER 44

The next day, fibres were found on the Skoda and further testing was being carried out to establish it was the same vehicle that killed Alison's first fiancé.

Now facing multiple charges, the hunt for Martin was stepped up. 'News at Ten' had asked for a photo, but Ruth said she only had a few snaps of her son as a boy.

He always avoids cameras she'd explained, but when they phoned Alison to see if she could help, it was David who took the call and he remembered how she'd sneaked a picture of him on her phone when they went kite surfing. It had captured Martin laughing so he looked quite different but, on the plus side, maybe his good looks would jog some memories.

Later that morning, David rang to get an update on Ben and was told that, sadly, he'd died in the night.

'We can't tell Alison about Richard now,' said David, after giving Fay the news. 'It'll be hard enough for her to cope with this, without having an ex-fiancé turn up on the doorstep.'

Fay took a tissue and dabbed her eyes. 'Yes, you're right,' she sniffed. 'Oh, that poor boy, how dreadful; I really hoped he'd pull through. We'll have to send a note to his parents.' Her eyes filled with tears again. 'They'll be devastated ... as will Alison ... Poor Alison; even though she knows it was Martin, she still feels responsible.'

Fay went off to break the news to her daughter while David phoned to tell Richard.

'The thing is, Alison is going to be in pieces when she hears about Ben and I don't think it's fair to add another complication to her life at the moment,' he said. 'Can you hang on a bit longer?'

'I guess so,' replied Richard. 'Actually, I've been using the time to do some thinking. I might have a crack at joining the police. I'm still eligible and have enough money to keep me comfortable for the rest of my life so it would be like a hobby really ... And I think I'd enjoy detective work. What do you think?'

'Well...' David paused, knocked back by the extent of Richard's wealth. 'Alison said you were interested when you were younger so if it's what you want to do, go for it.'

'I did wonder if I was too old, but I've checked and I'd still have a few years in the job once I've qualified. How d'you think Alison would feel about it?'

'I don't know,' said David cautiously. 'You'd have to ask her ... but not yet. I'll tell her about you when she's had time to come to terms with what's happened to Ben. By the way, Martin will be on 'News at Ten,' tonight.

CHAPTER 45

Martin lingered in the warmth of a pub for as long as he dared. Later he would return to the tent he'd dismantled and hidden that morning. Fortunately, it had stayed dry and he'd found a sheltered spot out of the wind, but he was aware he couldn't stay there indefinitely. He needed a plan, but so far had not come up with anything practical.

Was he worrying unnecessarily? Supposing Alison hadn't used her car. Perhaps she could just be wondering where he was ... in which case he could still make sure nothing bad happened to her; but how? To avoid the temptation of calling, he'd left his phone behind so had no way of warning her.

Just as he was finishing the pie and chips he'd ordered, his attention was drawn to a television behind the bar. Half hidden by a string of Christmas lights, it was on mute, but he'd been vaguely aware the news was on; and the picture now being displayed had him staring in disbelief because it was the one Alison had taken down on the beach a few weeks ago.

She'd laughed as she flashed her phone at him, proud that she'd managed to get a photo without him realising. It was a good likeness ... and secretly he'd been very pleased with it ... but now it was on TV, together with a telephone number.

So much for everything going away; the search for him was nation-wide. Behind frozen features, he fought back a surge of panic. No one appeared to be looking at the television, but he must get out now in case someone made the connection.

***

Ruth gazed at her son's face on the television without emotion. She couldn't recall the last time she'd seen him smile like that and speculated on how different life might have been had his father stayed with them and not become an alcoholic.

Thinking back to the day everything changed gave Ruth an idea of where Martin might be and, picking up the phone, she rang the number on the TV screen.

***

Matthew stared at the TV in amazement. There was no mistaking the young man laughing into the camera and he didn't need the caption underneath to tell him it was his son; apart from the happy face, he hadn't changed a bit.

But a man was talking over the picture. 'Wanted for questioning? ... May be dangerous ...

get in touch if you know where he is...'

When a phone number appeared, Matthew snatched up his pen to copy it onto the margin of a newspaper crossword he'd been tackling.

Just then, Sue came in with a cup of tea. 'Are you okay,' she asked?

Matthew glanced back to the screen, but the presenter had moved on to another story.

'Yes, fine.' A once familiar, but now rare wave of anger rose within him as he watched her go back to the kitchen. He'd behaved badly to Martin, of that he was painfully aware, but the boy had deserved it, upsetting his mother like that. He'd caused nothing but misery from the day he was born and it was because of him he'd lost Ruth.

However, the anger passed quickly leaving sorrow in its place, together with a growing recognition that perhaps as an absent father he ought to take a share of responsibility for whatever it was Martin was going through. And he had a gut feeling about where he might be.

Matthew rang the number and, after a brief conversation, grabbed his coat before shouting to Sue that he was going out. He drove a short distance, took a flashlight from the glove compartment and started to walk towards the place where he last saw his son, some fifteen years ago.

***

That's two people who think they know where

Landon may be hiding,' said the news co-ordinator as he passed on the details.

When the local police were alerted, they sent out a team immediately.

***

Martin's movements were almost robotic as he reconstructed the tent and threw in the duvet he'd picked up yesterday from a charity shop. It had kept out some of the cold but, despite his hardiness, camping in December was not his idea of fun.

In an effort to put the surreal moment of recognising himself on TV to one side, Martin found his thoughts straying back to a day he'd tried to erase from his memory. He'd been around eleven years old and it was the first time he'd completely lost control, the experience frightening him so badly that he never wanted to repeat it.

From then onwards, he'd battened down his feelings, hiding behind the façade he showed to the world; but, he continued to see the below the surface and occasionally the swirling emotions broke through.

It had almost happened in Docklands when, after wrecking the Porsche, he'd nearly stormed up to Richard's flat to tackle him with bare hands, regardless of the consequences.

Shuddering at the memories, he was smoothing out a second groundsheet inside the tent when a familiar voice him made him jump

convulsively and turn to face his visitor.
   'Hello son, I thought I might find you here.'

CHAPTER 46

Although Martin recognised the voice, he could only see the outline of a man waving a flashlight in his face.

'What have you been up to? I saw you on the news. Did you know you were famous?'

'Yes.' Martin felt strangely at peace. 'I saw it on a pub TV.'

'I know it's probably too late to tell you, but I do regret that I was such a useless father while you were growing up. Drink does bad things to you; but, I'm dry now ... have been since a week after that last time we were together. I stayed away though ... in case I was tempted again ... I honestly believed it was for the best.'

'How did you know I was here?'

'Because of what you said the day I left.'

Martin stayed silent. He'd known the answer before asking the question. It was for the same reason that he'd been drawn to buy the ticket at Victoria Station.

'You may only have been eleven, but you were deadly serious and I'm guessing you think this might be a way of resolving the crisis you've reached in your life.'

Martin didn't reply. Shouldn't he be feeling something ... anything other this unnatural calm?

'Incidentally, for your own safety I told the police where I thought you might be. Would it help to tell me what happened to bring you back here again? It must have been something pretty dreadful.'

This wasn't the father Martin remembered, but deep inside was a recollection of something warm and familiar ... a hazy memory of being very small ... of laughing as he was swung up in the air by strong arms, the wind rushing into his face ... of kicking a ball in the garden and of bedtime stories being read while he was wrapped cosily in a dressing gown. Maybe his father had been different when he was very young.

Martin had never let down his guard with anyone; even Alison didn't really know him; but, right now, he had a strong urge to unburden and it occurred to him that this man, no stranger to violence, might be the one person who would not judge him too harshly. And why shouldn't he be made to understand the consequences of his actions?

So, Martin took the groundsheet out of the tent and spread it on the grass outside and they both sat down. Then he began to tell his father everything that had happened since the last time they were together.

Matthew had been employing one of Sue's counselling tactics when he invited Martin to talk and soon regretted it when one story after another spilled out, his son becoming more animated as each unfolded.

He glanced across to the good-looking young man beside him, eerily lit by flashlights, and listened with growing horror, knowing he was at least partly responsible for all that had happened. If he'd been around perhaps he would have seen the anguish and somehow got through to his son.

'But why, did you do it?' he asked at one point.

Martin shrugged. 'Jealousy, I suppose. I don't make friends easily and when I do, I can't bear the thought of anyone else having them ... especially Alison. She left me once and it nearly destroyed me. I couldn't go through that again ... that's why I cut the brakes of her car before driving here.'

'Whhat?' Matthew was horrified all over again.

'I really love her, but she was slipping away and I had to do something. Otherwise I'd have lost her for the second time.'

'I don't understand ... if she dies, you'll have lost her anyway.'

'But don't you see? She'll still belong to me. She'll always be mine.'

Matthew shook his head in bewilderment and, just as he was wishing the television had been tuned to a different programme, two pools of light broke through the darkness and moved jerkily towards them.

Before Matthew could do anything, Martin jumped up and sprinted into the inky blackness. 'Don't try and stop me,' he shouted, 'I have to do this. We both know there's no going back after what I've done.'

Martin turned to face the sea, hesitated for a moment then fell from the cliff edge in a swallow dive.

The hungry waves were waiting to snatch him away, but this time he didn't wake up.

CHAPTER 47

Matthew had followed Martin to the edge of the cliff, but was too late to save his son. He'd failed again as a father and it was only Sue's untiring efforts that helped him resist the call of the bottle.

He told her everything about the last half-hour of Martin's life and she suggested it might help if he contacted Alison so he could share the pain with the woman Martin clearly loved.

At first Matthew refused. He'd already relayed Martin's confessions to the police. Surely that was enough. Besides, if he met Alison in Southcliffe, he ran the risk of running into Ruth and he couldn't bear the thought of that.

But, Sue didn't give up and gradually brought Matthew round to the idea of giving Alison the option of hearing his story. Get the police to ask her, she pleaded. She may say no, but at least you'll have tried and, either way, it will give you closure.

***

Soon after the Christmas and New Year festivities were over, Mike Bolton was given the job of passing on Matthew's proposition and, after talking it through with her parents, Alison agreed to meet Matthew on neutral ground away from Southcliffe.

Over coffee in a quiet café, Matthew went through everything that had happened during the last meeting with his son. Then, seeing Alison's bewilderment, he tried to make things clearer by telling her about the holiday they'd had in Eastbourne when Martin was eleven.

'On the whole, it had been a good week,' he began. 'We'd been out and about doing things to try and amuse Martin and I'd managed to stay off the drink, which was rare for me.' He looked across to Alison who still looked puzzled. 'Did Martin not tell you I was an alcoholic?'

Alison shook her head. 'No … in fact, I don't remember him ever mentioning you, to be honest.'

'Hmm … so he wrote me out of his life altogether then?'

Alison looked away. 'I assumed you and Ruth had separated. The truth is Martin didn't really talk about his home life at all. It was just the way he was, I suppose.'

'I see. Well, at this particular time, Ruth and I had been getting on better, but the trouble was, Martin hated it if we were happy…'

Alison raised her eyebrows. 'Go on.'

'On our last day, we went to Beachy Head … the same spot where I found him last month … and Martin was needling both of us.

'I tried to keep my temper, but he kept on goading until I finally exploded and told him exactly what I thought of him. The next thing I knew, he'd run to the edge of the cliff and was looking down at the sea.

'Don't be silly, I shouted. The gusts are strong. Come back or you'll fall.

'I could hardly hear Martin's reply through the howl of the wind. I won't fall, he yelled, I'll jump. There's no point in me being here because neither of you want me - you never have. I might as well dive in. Then I'll be out of your way forever.'

Matthew paused.

'I'd never seen Martin so angry; he stood there, swaying ... T-shirt billowing in the wind like a sail.

'I turned to Ruth for help and that's when the nightmare really began because she too had moved to the cliff edge a bit further along and was also looking down. I called her. Ruth! What are you doing? Move back. You'll get blown into the sea.

'I don't think I can stand this any longer, she shouted. Between the two of you, I'm at my wits end. What is the point of going on like this?'

Matthew had closed his eyes as he repeated her exact words.

'My wife and son could have been buffeted off the cliff at any second and both were threatening to jump. It was all down to me. That's what years of drinking had done to my family.'

In the silence that followed, Matthew thought back to the moment when there'd been a brief lull in the wind and he'd heard his son shout, 'One day I will jump off these cliffs and when I do, it'll be your fault?' But, he didn't relay that part to Alison.

'What happened next?'

Matthew brushed tears away with the back of his hand.

'There was a voice behind me ... a woman ... and she told me to step back. We need to get them away from the edge, she said, and I think it'll be easier to do that if you are out of their sight ...'

He paused again. It was so long since he'd allowed himself to re-live that day, yet everything remained so clear.

'When I turned, I saw more people ... they were wardens who patrol the cliffs to give help to the suicidal ... I started to walk away and as I glanced back, Ruth and Martin were being led to safety.

'The woman who'd spoken was following me ... trying to connect ... but I was beyond reach. I said I needed a drink ... and there was nothing she could do to prevent me from going on that week-long binge.'

Alison reached across the table and squeezed Matthew's hand.

He sighed. 'The warden's name was Sue and

she saved me. We're partners now and live together in Eastbourne.

'I can't pretend I was a good father ... apart from the very early years ... and it's likely my behaviour contributed to Martin turning out how he did. Had I been around, maybe I'd have noticed the signs and helped him manage his jealousy.'

'What about Martin's mother?' Alison's eyes shone with tears. 'Why didn't she help him?'

'I don't know ... probably couldn't reach him. Ruth had trouble bonding with Martin ... right from when he was a baby.'

'Poor Martin,' the tears spilled over. 'He must have been very unhappy.'

'Yes, I expect you're right,' said Matthew. 'And I'll never be free from the guilt of not being there for him.'

'You mustn't take all the blame,' Alison squeezed his hand again. 'Plenty of people have difficult childhoods, but they don't go round killing people who upset them. There's always the element of choice and Martin started going off course when he tried to get rid of his school friend, Tim.

'Also, Martin was at his happiest by the sea; you could say it was his element of choice as well; so maybe that's why he chose to end his life there when it all got too much.'

'That's one way of looking at it I suppose,' said Matthew. 'Anyway, my demons are not your problem. Martin told me he loved you and, as much as anyone could, I think you made him happy.

'But, there's nothing you can do for him now. You have your whole life ahead so you must try and put this behind you.'

Later that day, Matthew went back to Sue, resolving to try and follow his own advice.

***

David had dropped Alison off for the meeting with Matthew and was waiting outside the café to take her home.

In the car, she told her father everything, finishing with the bit about Matthew advising her to move on and continue with her life.

David was shocked to hear the full story. 'Well, at least we know now why Martin had issues,' he said. 'Clearly he'd been through a miserable childhood, but Matthew was right, you have to draw a line. Studying will help ... and you have your new career to look forward to.

'Incidentally, your mother and I haven't said anything until now because of all that's been going on, but Richard came down the day of your accident. He was worried about you ... in fact he was the one who was concerned that Martin might turn on you. Did you know he was interested in psychology?'

Alison made no comment and continued to stare out of the window.

'He went home about six weeks ago ... the day Martin died actually ... because he thought it better to wait until things settled down. But he wants to see you ... and he's thinking about joining the police force.'

Unable to hide her surprise, Alison turned to her father. 'You're joking? ... He'll never give up his beloved city life.'

'Well, he mentioned something about age catching up; perhaps he wants to get out while he's still on top. And I think if you were interested, he would consider moving down this way to do his training. He really wants to talk to you. Why don't you think about it?

'He's changed since you first brought him home ... looks at life differently now. You might be pleasantly surprised.'

TWO AND A HALF YEARS LATER

It was a beautiful summer day when Alison walked down the aisle on her father's arm to meet her groom, PC Clancy.

Richard had long since discarded the Docklands flat, together with his young girlfriend, and had been living with Alison, now a teacher, about five miles away from Southcliffe.

David was right; Richard had changed. Alison noticed it straightaway although she'd been cautious about renewing their relationship. But, Richard was patient and also had a new career on which to focus.

He'd grown in confidence as well as maturity and, by the time he'd qualified, Alison was sure he was the man she wanted to marry.

Outside the church, Richard gazed at his new wife and the love in his eyes was there for all to see. He knew he was lucky. He'd lost Alison for a while, but ghosts from the past had finally been laid to rest and now, they could look forward to the next chapter of their lives together.

***

Made in the USA
Middletown, DE
16 April 2025